The Enchanted Shadow-verse Saga

Presents

THE DHAMPYRE CHRONICLES

INTO THE NIGHT

Q.T. Barrett

1

Vampire [vam-pahyuh r]

Demonic creatures who live off of the blood of humans; a vampire appears to be a normal person until the thirst is upon them and only then, do they reveal their true demonic visage. They possess superhuman strength, speed, agility, as well as heightened senses far beyond the reach of a normal human being. Vampires are highly allergic to garlic, customized metallic silver, and sunlight. They exist and are confined to the shadows of the night. Vampires are solely dedicated to the thirst for blood and the advancement of their species.

Blood Sabers

A half-human and half-vampire hybrid. A Saber is generally one with all or most strengths of a vampire, with few to no disadvantages. Blood Sabers are known to quite often reject their vampire blood and became extremely successful vampire hunters due to their hybrid physiology and advanced abilities. However, despite their contributions to the human race, they were continually rejected, nonetheless, because of their vampire blood. Thus, Sabers most always spent their life as nomads, rejected by both humans and vampires. Blood Sabers, like their vampiric predecessors, can create and spawn more of their own species through fang-to-flesh contact. However, the hybrid strain is even more exclusive than vampires.

- o The Hybrid/Saber strain of the vampire virus causes similar biological changes in the host endowing them with heightened senses and greatly augmented para-physical capabilities.

- o Like their predecessors (the vampire race), Hybrid Immortals possess superhuman physical abilities, including strength, speed, agility, reflexes, and endurance. Their physical abilities increase with age.

Re-occurrences
Human beings who have experienced transmigration or metempsychosis, also known as reincarnated individuals. Re-occurrences often resemble a similar, if not the same physical appearance from one lifetime to the next. Re-occurrences are often known as "Echos."

N.I.G.H.T.F.A.L.L
The **N**octurnal **I**nitiative of **G**overned **H**eightened **T**errestrial(s), and Factions of Advanced, Lawful Logistics

   o An extra-governmental counter-terrorism intelligence agency charged with monitoring paranormal, supernatural, occult, and rogue technologies. The agency maintains strong relations to various branches of the Armed Forces, however, it is a private organization that receives funding from several major governments, such as the United States, the United Kingdom, Canada, Germany, and Japan.

   o Founded in the wake of □ □ ⊞ N.I.G.H.T.F.A.L.L. has continued to monitor and deal with the significant rise in para-cursed augmented individuals, paranormal occurrences, and dangerous rogue technologies.

PARANORMAL DEFENSE INITIATIVE OF 2021

- In response to the world growing stranger by the minute, the governments of the world passed a bill that enacted the *"Paranormal Defense Initiative."*

- The PDI was designed to establish agencies dedicated to monitoring and policing individuals with supernatural and paranormal abilities both foreign and domestic. In America, two paranormal response agencies were created called, *"VESSEL and N.I.G.H.T.F.A.L.L" regime.* They often enlisted the help of para-enhanced agents and unique individuals with supernatural abilities who could be trusted to preserve humanity and act as a bridge between the natural world and the paranormal. The Paranormal Defense Initiative also required individuals with paranormal abilities to register with government entities to make all agencies known to their existence. This plan would serve as the best line of defense against the weird and wicked or so everyone thought…

TABLE OF CONTENTS

Prologue

It was the scariest night of my life. The rain lashed against the windows, as the wind swept through our family estate. Although our home could weather the forces of nature, a paralyzing chill came over my tiny frame. Bewildered, I watched my parents prepare to vacate our house in the middle of the night. As the lightning cut through the darkness, the unyielding thunder followed. With every shocking uproar, my body trembled with fear. My father paced frantically about his study. He gathered lots of books and mysterious papers, stuffing them into his leather briefcase. Dad's chalkboard was completely bare. It was very uncommon to not see his scribble all over it. There was an anxious expression on his face. He noticed me standing in the doorway. "Son, go find your mother," he insisted. Without a moment's hesitation, I ran to my parents' bedroom. My mother was busy gathering our belongings. What had my parents so terrified? More importantly, why were we leaving our home during a raging storm? I was never a fan of this big, scary house to begin with. We lived on the outskirts of town, deep in the country and there wasn't a soul for miles. Our land was vast. "What was coming for us?" I asked myself.

The lights began to flicker, adding to the horror of it all. Was the storm paving the way for a terrible incoming? As mom finished packing, my father grabbed me by my shoulders and kneeled. He spoke firmly, "Lucas, I know you're afraid and don't understand the course of events transpiring at this moment. In time, everything will become clear. When that day comes, you and only you will have the power to reshape the world. Remember, I love you and your true power lies here." He pointed at my chest and proudly placed his pendant around my neck. He gently kissed my forehead, as if it would be the last time we would see each other. Tears began to cloud my eyes. There were so many unanswered questions, as fear continued to build, and my heart raced.

As my mother approached the door with our luggage, the lights flickered off. My father whispered nervously, "It's too late." He rushed to unlock the side door by the stairs and removed two fully automatic, assault rifles. My mother positioned me behind her before kneeling to kiss me and whispered, "I love you, baby." She stood up and took a ready-firing position, along with my father.

I was startled by the thunderous banging on the front door. My mother and father did a complete about-

face and prepared to fight for our lives. The banging echoed throughout the house. I had never been so frightened, and my entire body froze. I tried to scream but couldn't. My heart fluttered uncontrollably. Suddenly, multiple intruders burst through the door and windows. Without hesitation, my mother and father began unloading gunfire.

1

The Dark Stranger

After a vivid, horrifying nightmare of his parents' death, Lucas awakened in his apartment covered in sweat. For the last fifteen years, he could never fully complete this recurring dream. Lucas reached for his anxiety medication to calm his mind and noticed the time. He quickly got dressed and grabbed his books for class. Like his father, Lucas has a passion for the sciences, majoring in Biology with a concentration in Evolutionary Genetics.

He sat in class completely out of focus. His mind wondered back to his nightmare. The violent flashes were becoming more and more frequent. Bloody images were beginning to manifest, even while he was awake. Lucas couldn't help but wonder if these were suppressed memories from his childhood. He quickly grabbed his books and stormed out during the professor's lecture. He sat alone, rooted in fear. He closed his eyes, hoping to block out the images.

Overwhelmed with frustration, he felt parts of his memory had been erased. He opened his eyes and noticed an attractive woman across campus. Suddenly, he's distracted by a horde of students leaving class. He looked up and the woman was gone.

His cell phone vibrated. It was his grandfather, the great Colonel Mason Shaw. Lucas answered sarcastically, "Hello Colonel, how is your day going?"

"I am well, buddy. How are your classes?" His grandfather asked. "My classes are fine. I just wish I could sleep a little better, that's all," Lucas answered.

"You're still having those nightmares? Are you taking your anxiety medication?" The Colonel asked. "Yes and yes," Lucas stated.

"It's not uncommon to experience flashes of death and violence. Many elite soldiers, like yourself, suffer from post-traumatic stress. Hell, I've even experienced it. Some of that stuff is bound to stay with us. Perhaps, you should speak with your psychiatrist," the Colonel suggested.

"Granddaddy, the flashes I'm experiencing are from my childhood. It's not battle stress. To be more specific, it's a frightful memory from the night my parents died," Lucas explained. The Colonel paused, as if he knew exactly what his grandson was referring to. Lucas sensed his grandfather was gas-lighting, refusing to offer details surrounding the death of his parents. After a few more minutes of chit-chat, Lucas decided to head to the campus gym for a short workout before his highly anticipated fight. Secretly, Lucas participates in an underground Mixed Martial Arts fighting circuit. He occasionally fights to keep extra money in his pocket. The Colonel had him train with multiple military specialists in the Arts of Combat, since the age of six. Before Lucas could read, he was learning combative tactics, and the many ways to kill.

Lucas pulled up to the parking lot on his Ducati motorcycle, noticing lots of cars assembled in a circle. The entire lot was packed with people chanting, cheering and yelling. Lucas made his way to the crowd, totally unaware he's being watched by mysterious men cloaked in darkness. He walked over to greet the promoter. Some of the students recognized him, as he entered the ring. After exchanging a few words, the promoter delivered his speech, hyping up the audience.

"Ladies and gents. Tonight we have royalty among us. Give an extra warm welcome to Mr.

Punishment himself! He is the mighty...the gladius warrior of precision and elegance like you've never seen! A man who has never known defeat. I give you the formidable Mrrrrrr. Shawwwww! And In this corner, we have his challenger, mister large and in charge. I present to you the S-L-E-D-G-E H-A-M-M-E-R!!!"

Lucas began focusing on his opponent. He sized up his weaknesses and openings. Sledgehammer warmed up by kicking through targeting pads and shields. As both men approached front and center and touched fists, Sledgehammer was highly overconfident standing toe-to-toe with Lucas. He looked Sledgehammer in his eyes, displaying a calm, quiet confidence. Letting his opponent know he wasn't afraid. As they retreated to their corners, Sledgehammer chanted, "Tonight, punishment will be served." As they began fighting, Lucas evaded Sledgehammer's strikes and wasn't fazed by the ones he landed. He strategically moved about, hitting with devastating blows to places Sledgehammer found hard to recover. This increased Hammer's anger, which made it easier for Lucas to take him apart. He ended the fight with an explosive, spinning, spread-eagle kick to Sledgehammer's head. He fell, face first onto the concrete pavement. The countdown began and continued with Hammer still on the pavement bleeding profusely from his face. The crowd raved and cheered, totally amazed by what they had witnessed. The promoter came over and grabbed Lucas by the arm and raised it high, symbolizing him as victor of the fight. With five hundred dollars in hand and not a scratch on him, Lucas left. The crowd was still applauding as he walked away. His unbelievable fighting skills left everyone in awe. He was almost God-like.

As he approached his bike, he noticed the same beautiful woman who caught his eye outside of the science building. For a brief moment, their eyes connected, as if they were familiar with each other. Maybe they knew the same forbidden secret. Once again, she vanished. Baffled by this second disappearing act, Lucas gathered himself and left the premises.

Arriving at his apartment, Lucas was still unaware he was being followed. Quickly, he jumped in the shower, excited about a party he was attending downtown. As he dressed, his mind wondered back to the mysterious woman. She was around five feet, five inches tall with thick, ebony hair and smooth, chocolate skin. Lucas couldn't help but fantasize about her curvaceous body. She was top-heavy with a figure-eight shape. His mouth watered, as a feeling of familiarity came over him. He quickly shook it off as being ludicrous and impossible. He jumped on his motorcycle and left for the party.

He arrived at the club around 10:30 p.m. just before the line began to wrap around the building. Lucas was well-acquainted with the promoters and bouncers, so he strolled right in. He showed some love to his friends and greeted the club owners. Continuing to shake hands, he headed to the bar. He ordered his drink of choice, a Royal Flush with a shot of Washington Apple. Lucas posted up, observing as the club filled with people. Tons of beautiful women, dressed extravagantly from head to toe, flooded the scene. Lucas remained very laid-back, while sipping his drink. His fellow associates began praising him on his victory against Sledgehammer. Lucas thanked them and commenced to getting his dance on. He was sandwiched between two lovely girls, interested in taking him home for the night. However, his mind remained occupied by the mystery woman. Then, he spotted her. She strolled in with a group of people Lucas assumed were her friends. He was instantly entranced by her beauty, but at the same time, he wondered which guy was her lover. Their eye color

14

struck Lucas as unusual. Each of them possessed gold-colored irises, which accentuated their flawless, brown skin. They walked in like they owned the place. Everyone knew them, as if they were Hollywood celebrities.

She looked over in Lucas's direction and paused. Their eyes met. Lucas made his way to the bar and continued to gaze at her, while other interested guys sought her attention. He ordered another shot of Washington Apple. Lucas tossed back the shot and made his way to the restroom. When he looked back in her direction, she was gone. Suddenly, he noticed she was dancing with some random, thirsty-ass dude. The girl had skills. She danced with grace, yet her moves were sexy and very enticing. She had the body of a goddess and she knew it. Looking for an easy lay, the guy offered to take her home to play. She whispered, "I'm flattered, but I'm not interested and I play a little rough." Leaving her partner with a hard-on and a loss for words, she continued to zoom-in on what truly interested her. She gazed into Lucas's eyes as he passed. Feeling somewhat indifferent about this mysterious woman dancing with another guy, Lucas broke their eye contact. There was a connection between them that left him perplexed. He never felt this crazy about anyone, especially a stranger. He washed and dried his hands, then left the restroom. There she was, leaning against the wall, seductively. Lucas was surprised by her presence. He was also shocked by her ability to sniff out his exact locations.

"Can I help you?" He asked.

"Well, I certainly hope so, handsome. I was wondering if you were going to avoid me all night or ask me to dance," she replied.

"Oh really, I thought you'd already found a partner," Lucas stated.

She smiled, while avoiding his answer. She continued to stare Lucas down for a solid minute as if she were mesmerized by the very sight of him. Her gaze was disturbing, yet incredibly seductive.

"What are you staring at?" He asked.

"Do I make you uncomfortable?" She asked, approaching Lucas in a very intimate manner.

"No. That's not exactly the word I would use," Lucas stated, feeling her body press up against his.

"Perhaps I see something I like. Forgive my manners, my name is Lori Slade, but you can call me Lo," she stated.

She extended her pretty hand. Lucas gently shook it and responded, "It's nice to meet you, Lo. My friends call me Luc."

"I get the strangest feeling we've met before," Lucas said.

"Maybe, in another life. Do you believe in the supernatural?" Lori asked, dropping subtle hints she knew Lucas wouldn't understand.

"I don't know. The world is a strange place. Sometimes, I feel things exist beyond my understanding," Lucas replied.

"I know exactly what you mean," she said, moving a litter closer.

"Would you like to dance?" He asked.

"Well, it's about damn time you asked a sister to dance," Lori joked.

"I'm not the type to wait in line," Lucas stated, referring to her other dance partner. Lori's excitement made her moist, as she nibbled on her bottom lip.

17

Lucas took her by the hand and maneuvered their way to the dance floor. Lori's crew stared, in disapproval. They danced close and provocatively, as if everyone had vanished. Lucas smelled the delicious scent of her body and hair. Her dark blue jeans, accentuated her curves. She sported a low-cut, black tank-top that hugged her breasts nicely. The fragrance she wore was perfect. She didn't shower herself in perfume like some women. It was sweet and natural. While dancing, they stared into each other's eyes. It was truly a moment of perfection. As the DJ was spinning the perfect slow track, she began to grind slowly against Lucas. Taking him by the hand, she led him to the back wall, where the club was darkest. Ignoring her crew, Lori pressed her lovely body up against him. She was grinding against his large bulge, as he held her hips. Face to face, but never kissing nor saying a word, they reveled with sheer passion.

Breathing heavily, she whispered in his ear, "Do you like this?"

"Yes," Lucas replied, as she caressed him between his legs.

"Do you like me?" Lori whispered.

"Yes," Lucas replied, breathing heavily and not wanting her to stop.

"Do you want me? Say it...say you want me," Lori demanded seductively.

Toward the end of the song, Lori's crew signaled they were leaving. She gave Lucas a sweet kiss on the cheek and said, "I have to go."

As she turned to leave, Lucas gently grabbed her by the hand and said, "Wait. Can I get your number?"

She replied gazing into his eyes, "I will find you. I promise."

He continued to stare, as she left the club. Interestingly, Lori's crew was her adopted siblings. One being her blood-sister, Nezera, who asked, "Was that the guy?"

Lori grabbed her coat. "Nez, why ask questions, if you already know the answers?" She asked.

"Little sister, we have to tread lightly. We have no time to focus on your reincarnated love affair," Nez replied.

"Nez, remember who you're talking to. We have lived many lifetimes and I'm a lot wiser than you think. I don't need you to protect or chastise me. I am quite capable of looking out for myself," Lori stated.

As they conversed in the middle of the street, surrounded by their male siblings, darkness fell upon them. Lori and Nezera were escorted by their two foster brothers, Alexander and Jeremiah. Nezera and Jeremiah were not only foster brother and sister. They are husband and wife, which made Jeremiah Lori's brother in-law.

The four of them disappeared into the night. Shortly afterwards, Lucas left the club with a sly grin on his face and a bulging hard-on. On his way to his apartment, he could not stop thinking of Lori. Even as he slept, his mind wandered back to the club scene. He fantasized about the way they danced, her delicious scent and the way she moved. Although, Lucas had no way of reaching her, he knew somehow, they would meet again. The very next day, he entered Professor Grant's genetics class. She was a beautiful, caramel-skinned woman who was always very polite and humble. She was incredibly brilliant, as well as, wise. However, she had a strange way of looking at Lucas when he approached her about assignments and study sessions. He often wondered about her expressions.

After Lucas left the science building, he walked around campus hoping to run into Lori. He continued this same routine for weeks, but his mystery woman could not be found. On Friday, as Lucas was leaving one of his classes, there she was...standing in front the Student Union building. She stared him down with the same seductive, tortured gaze she had the night they met. Again, it was as if she knew the exact place where he would be.

"I told you I would find you," she said.

Lucas was surprised to see her after a few weeks of no contact.

"I was beginning to think you reconnected with an old lover or something," he stated sarcastically. Although Lucas was spot on, it was more complicated than he could've ever imagined.

She looked into his eyes and said with a smirk, "You have no idea."

"Well, Ms. Mysterious, would you like to take a walk with me?" He asked. She smiled and grabbed the inside of his arm. As they strolled through campus, Lucas began asking Lori some personal questions.

"Are you a student? Where are you from? What's your major? Where did you disappear to?"

Lori managed to avoid him, deflecting to questions of her own. Lucas became even more interested in pursuing her. While sitting in the cafeteria, Lucas asked one final question, "If you don't mind me asking, is that your real eye color?" At first, she hesitated to answer, but looked up and said, "Yes, these are my actual eyes." She quickly looked away and changed the subject.

"Why do you do it? Why do you fight?" She asked.

"Oh wow. So, you've been following me?" Lucas asked, knowing she had.

"Is there a problem?" Lori asked.

"Well, that depends on your intentions. Funny, there aren't many people who can sneak up on me," He stated.

"After my parents were killed, my grandfather had me train with various specialists around the world.

After graduating high school, I enlisted in the Armed Forces and for a while, I was good at it. Some even considered me a God among soldiers. But in the end, I wanted more for my life than being a gifted killer. Certain habits from that life stuck with me. I fight to quench a familiar thirst and it's as simple as that. So, I use my skills to make a little money," Lucas said.

"You said your parents were killed. What happened?" Lori asked.

"Honestly, I don't know. I don't have a lot of memories of my parents. My grandfather, The Colonel, would have me believe that they died in a car accident or some fabricated bullshit like that. But, I'm afraid my early years and the death of my parents are shrouded in mystery," Lucas explained.

"Why do you say fabricated? Do you not believe him?" Lori asked.

"My grandfather is a military Colonel. Let's just say, keeping secrets is what he does for a living. Government and International Relations has been his career for almost fifty years," Lucas stated.

"I know how you feel and I'm so sorry. My sister and I were orphaned at a very young age and for a long time, it was just the two of us," Lori recalled.

"Wow, the vibe is getting way too deep right now," she said.

Lori gazed at Lucas eating lunch, totally amazed by every single movement he made. Lucas noticed she wasn't eating, but he kept it to himself.

"What are your plans for tonight?" She asked.

"I have none...why? Are you trying to tuck me in for the evening?" Lucas flirted.

Again, Lori gazed into him, not giving an immediate answer. She leaned very close and whispered, "Let's get out of here."

They quickly left the cafeteria and sped to their destination. As soon as they reached the door of Lucas's apartment, things were on and popping. There was lots of kissing, heavy breathing, and clothes flying off. Lori shoved Lucas onto his bed and stripped down to nothing. For a moment, Lucas noticed the tribal markings tattooed on her shoulders, back and forearms. She then climbed on top, straddling him as

24

she kissed his lips. Lucas grabbed her by the hips and reversed their position, laying Lori on her back. He quickly removed his pants and boxers and continued kissing her in all the right places. He spread her legs and with his tongue, he gently licked the hood of her clit. Lori's body bucked from pleasure as Lucas licked her sweet nectar and tugged on her bush.

Lori saw Lucas's package and was amazed by his girth. She was eager to take him into her mouth. She did not hesitate to reciprocate, throwing neck as Lucas became overwhelmed with pleasure. She proceeded to put her arms around his neck, pulling him in for a passionate kiss. Slowly entering inside her, Lucas kept his eyes focused on her. She squealed with exhilarated passion. He knew exactly how to satisfy Lori with long, deep strokes. As she moaned, mind-blowing orgasms manifested her fierce, hybrid features. Her fingernails elongated, leaving numerous scratches on Lucas's back. Positioning her face near his neck, Lori's canines enlarged, and her eyes amplified into an even brighter, amber hue. Lori spotted the veins and yearned to sink her fangs into them, but she quickly flipped Lucas onto his back, while transforming her hybrid features to a relaxed state. She continued to ride Lucas with every intention of making him erupt and erupted, he did. He stared into her eyes, moaning loudly as he climaxed. Then, Lori slowed to a gentle grind.

Breathing heavily, she asked, "Are you always this kinky?"

"No, I just haven't had the touch of a good woman in a long while," Lucas said.

"What makes you think I'm good?" She asked smiling.

Lori gave Lucas an innocent stare and kissed him deeply. He flipped her over, as he got his second wind and they went at it for another round…or two.

2

Fire in the Night

Elsewhere, in the shadows of the night, a gathering took place. Revealing themselves in the light, you could see their figures with pale skin, fierce blue eyes and overgrown canines. Out of the darkness, a man appeared dressed in a long, black draping coat. He also possessed animal-like features.

"Have you located the boy?" He asked.

"Yes Dorian, we have. He attends the university nearby," the female answered.

"Good. I want to know his exact whereabouts for tomorrow night. We will take him quietly and I want no mistakes," he ordered.

Each of them nodded with approval. Immediately, they turned their attention to a couple walking through the park. Dorian and his group of cold-blooded, ferocious bloodsuckers saw this innocent couple. Their mouths began to water.

At first, they toyed with the couple causing the man to beg for the woman's life. At the blink of an eye, they pounced and hungrily feasted on the young woman's flesh. She began to die slowly, while the young man watched in horror, screaming for his love. Dorian grabbed the man and violently pulled his head to the side.

"Love is for the weak! Nothing more than livestock!" Dorian yelled, then tore his teeth into the man's neck.

The next morning, Lucas awakened to the sound of a loud, startling ringtone. The beaming sunlight made it impossible to stay in bed. Lucas rolled over and Lori was gone. Her lace panties still on the floor. She left a note which read, *"Just a little reminder of my sweetness."* He assumed she left in the middle of the night. Lucas's phone continued to ring as he quickly rolled over to answer it. The caller ID on his phone read Jackson Horton, Lucas's friend and mentor. "What up Jack?" Lucas answered. "Hey man, are you teaching at the studio tonight?" He asked.

Lucas gathered his thoughts trying to recall if he had made any previous plans.

"Yeah man, I'll be there at seven," Lucas answered.

On certain weeknights and weekends, Lucas trains a small group on the many disciplines of Martial Arts. He trains students in the Arts of Jujutsu, Karate, Taekwondo, Eskrima, and Wing Chun Kung Fu.

Lucas reflected on his night with Lori and how she made him feel.

"Where could she have fled to?" He wondered.

Mystery was a part of their awkward relationship and Lucas could not shake it. "Who is this amazing woman?" He said to himself.

Unbeknownst to Lucas and the rest of humanity, Lorelei Slade, referring to herself as Lo, is a Saber Siren. She is a member of an elite hybrid clan that is neither human nor vampire, but an infusion of both. Lo has existed for hundreds of years as one of many immortal, hybrid-infused hunters tipping the balance in the favor of mankind against the evil, bloodsucking demons of the night. She resides with her family and

coven, the Slades, also known as the "Silver Fangs".
They are one of many powerful, hybrid covens existing
between the worlds of men and vampires. Each hybrid
possesses the same strength and physicality of a
vampire, without the usual weaknesses to sunlight,
silver and garlic. Their human and vampire-physiology
causes them to constantly be at odds with their own
natures. The Slades estate is on the edge of town
surrounded by dense woods. They reside in an
immaculate, three-story, contemporary-style home. It
has six spacious bedrooms and a uniquely designed
pool and jacuzzi.

As the sun sets and the sky begins to darken,
Lori pulls up to the house in her black Lexus. Upon
entering, she's approached by her adoptive father,
Joshua. The patriarch of the family, leader of the
Slade Clan, and a very powerful hybrid immortal.

"Lo, come with me. There's something I think
you should see," Joshua demanded.

She followed him into the family briefing room
where the rest of the family awaited the news of
immediate danger. The room contained various forms
of future tech, including an Interactive Holographic
Interface. Joshua began briefing the family. He

manipulated the interface to display a holographic visual of a very dangerous Blood Immortal named Dorian Ross.

As his family gave their full attention, Joshua warned, "We have a very serious problem. Dorian Ross is lurking around town."

Alexander asked, "What is he after?"

Joshua turned his head towards Lori and changed the holographic display to a visual of Lucas.

"He is after your human-reoccurrence", Joshua stated.

"Why? What does he want with him?" Lori asked.

"Captain Lucas Thomas Shaw, born February 19th, 1992 in Houston, Texas to Dr. Richard and Imeena Shaw. At age five, after relocating to the family's estate in South Carolina, both parents are brutally murdered in the night by what the authorities claimed to be an animal attack. The boy's grandfather, Colonel Omar Shaw took him in and after graduating from high school, he enlisted into the military. He's done various tours in just about every third-world

hellhole you can image...Iraq, Iran, Afghanistan, Pakistan, North Korea, and Jakarta. Eventually, he joined a Shadow-Ops, think-tank group where he adopted the name Killcount. At one point, this guy was a one-man strike team. Single-handedly undermining military units and rogue regimes all on his own. His specialty was ambush operations, explosives, and subterfuge. Some regarded him as a God among soldiers. Two years ago, he walked away from it all and enrolled as a college student here in town", Abigail explained.

"Lucas Shaw is much more than you think, he's not just your beloved reincarnate. Ross plans to set a trap for him and we need to intercept him quickly before that happens. Lo, you have his scent...track Lucas's location and get him here fast," Joshua urged.

"No need, we are tracking him now," Abigail interjected.

Lori turned and left in a hurry. She went to her room and grabbed a long, black, wooden case from her closet and opened it with extreme care. It was a sharp-bladed weapon with a long silver chain that resembled a modified Kyoketsu Shoge. It was covered in a thick, red cloth made of velvet.

As Lori removed the cloth to reveal the weapon, Nezera entered.

"It's happening, isn't it? The prophecy is upon us and here you are, willing to risk everything, yet again," Nezera said.

"You heard Joshua. There's more to Lucas than we realized and when I bring him back, we will find out what that is," Lori explained.

"Bullshit, little sister. You can't fool me. Don't pretend this is just business, as usual. You fucked him, didn't you? I already know. I can smell the very scent of him all over you...you're already caught up. You should really be careful and leave your emotions out of this. Dorian Ross is one of the most dangerous, renegade blood-lords within the Blood Sovereign," Nezera declared.

"Nez, I need no reminder of who we're dealing with and you've never given a damn about who I was fucking before," Lori stated.

"Well, we all know this isn't just some random fuck you needed to get out of your system," Nezera responded.

"This is nothing new, Nez. We all knew this day was coming and I've been waiting for over two hundred years. Dear sister, why can't you respect that I desire intimacy like the rest of you?" Lorelei asked.

Nezera pulled Lori close, hugged her tightly and said, "Of course I want that for you. I've always wanted that for you, but you deserve someone who's willing to risk it all...just as you did."

Nez urged Lori to be careful, as she quickly made her way down the steps without breaking stride. Joshua waited at the front door. "Be careful Lo," he stated and wrapped his arms around her.

"Yes father," Lori assured.

"I've always trusted you and that will never waiver, but I could use a bit more information. What did you mean when you said he's much more?" Lori asked.

"Bring Lucas to me and I promise, it will all be revealed," Joshua said.

Lori gave Joshua a quick kiss on the cheek and jumped into her car. She aided Joshua's word and began tracking Lucas's scent. Anyone connected to the vampire bloodline, possessed acute senses and heightened depth perception...beyond that of any human. This made the immortal, hybrid race extremely difficult to challenge.

Later that evening, Lucas completed another seminar at his studio. He decided to stick around after class, training and punching on the bag.

"Wow, you're definitely releasing some frustration there, pal," Jackson stated.

As they closed the studio, Lucas confided in Jackson, "I'm kind of seeing this girl, but I don't know what to make of her. Last night, we had some intense, mind-blowing sex. She was amazing, but when I rolled over this morning, she was gone...disappeared with a quickness. She always seems to vanish when things are getting good. I wish I knew why."

"Patience is your most valuable asset when it comes to women, bro. Eventually their true motives become very clear. So, how does this mystery woman look?" Jackson asked.

Lucas began to describe Lori in full detail, as they headed toward the parking lot.

"I know absolutely nothing about this girl. She's a complete mystery," Lucas claimed.

"Well bro, be careful. Truth and secrets come with a huge price. It's entirely your decision to continue allowing her to drop in and out of your life. Hopefully, she'll reveal the full story," Jackson explained.

Jackson continued to give Lucas advice, as they approached their cars. After a lengthy conversation about relationships, he gave Lucas a hug, then drove off. Long after Jackson left, Lucas lingered in the parking lot reflecting on the events of his life. He began to realize that Lori could never be who he wanted. There were more than enough secrets lingering within Lucas's existence. He decided he would no longer object himself to the secrets of others. He jumped on his bike and pulled off with a new perspective. Suddenly, he remembered to pick up his anxiety medication from the pharmacy.

Lucas arrived at Walgreens, parked his bike, and removed his helmet. He entered the store and headed to the Pharmacy. As he approached the register, two individuals waited in front of him. Lucas quickly noticed a pale man dressed in dark clothing.

The man approached him and said his full name, "Lucas Shaw."

"I'm sorry, do I know you?" Lucas asked.

The man instantly grabbed him by the throat and lifted Lucas ten inches off the floor with ease. People began to flee in fear, realizing the situation was becoming very hostile. Lucas struggled, while trying to loosen the man's grip, but his strength was too overpowering.

"What do you want?" Lucas gasped.

"Your blood, your flesh is different," the man answered.

His horrifying, demonic features manifested. As the bloodsucker's grip strengthened, Lucas's will to stay conscious began to diminish. Suddenly, there were gun shots. Instantly, the vampire disintegrated into fiery ash as Lucas fell to the floor. People were running for cover, scattering like roaches. Lucas regained consciousness and focused on his surroundings. Although his vision was blurry, he could see an hourglass figure approaching him. She was holding a modified, sawed-off shot gun. As clear as day, he knew it was her. The mysterious woman had come to his rescue. Shocked and dazed, Lucas whispered her name, "Lori?" She grabbed him by the arm and lifted Lucas to his feet. Unexpectedly, more vampires quickly converged on their position, surrounding them. Lori dispatched two more them with fierce gunshots. Lucas watched as the bodies of her targets incinerated and reduced to charred piles of ash. Lori was manifesting daggers and various blades out of thin air. She single-handedly took out her attackers one by one, impaling and tossing bodies into the aisles of the store.

"Here, take this and cover me," she ordered.

Lori pulled out her chained weapon. She began whipping, slinging and stabbing. While utilizing her superior combat skills, she laid waste to more vicious bloodsuckers in her path. Lucas quickly began blasting a vampire moving erratically through the aisles. He had never seen anything move like these creatures. They were able to scale surfaces, climb walls and adhere to ceilings. He didn't have much luck because of the way they maneuvered. Their patterns were extremely unpredictable. Lori quickly intervened before the vicious vampire fully converged upon Lucas. She utilized a silver throwing projectile, launching it into the vampire's windpipe before reaching Lucas. Blood gushed from the bloodsucker's throat as he dropped to his knees, clenching his neck. Fiery blue ash emanated from the wound and covered his entire vessel. Lucas stared in total shock and disbelief.

Lori quickly grabbed Lucas, made their way toward the door, and into the parking lot. They were immediately fired upon by more vampires with automatic rifles. Lori covered Lucas, as she returned fire.

"Get in the car!" She ordered.

"I don't know your car, woman…which one?" Lucas responded.

"The black Lexus!" Lori shouted.

He rushed to the Lexus and dove into the front passenger side. Lori continued to return fire as she made her way to the car. She quickly jumped in, cranked the ignition and drove off.

"What the fuck is happening?" Lucas asked, clearly frustrated.

Lori sped pass the police cars that were responding to the 911 calls of shots fired. The police were traveling in such a grand haste, they unknowingly passed Lori's vehicle. Crouched down in the front seat, Lucas had the most horrified look on his face.

"Who the fuck were those ghouls and how did you turn them to ash like that?" Lucas asked breathing heavily.

"Lucas, I'm not really in a position to explain what's happening right now. Let's just say, life is much darker and stranger than you know. You live in a world where myth, legend and nightmares are real," Lori stated. She then looked him straight in his eyes and said, "Vampires."

"What?" Lucas asked in disbelief.

"Oh, come on. You already witnessed mister happy fangs back at the store," Lori replied.

He began thinking back on what he had witnessed, while desperately trying to make sense of it all.

"Lucas, you have been targeted for capture," Lori informed.

"Why...why me?" He asked.

"I don't know, Lucas. Please let me focus on the road and getting you to a location without compromising our safety," Lori stated firmly.

All of a sudden, there was a violent impact from the rear. Rapid gunfire ensued and Lori's back window was blasted out. The large SUV filled with hostile, hideous bloodsuckers was locked and loaded with assault rifles. Lucas's instincts took over, as he cocked the modified shotgun and fired back. The chase continued throughout the inner city. Lori insisted he steer the wheel, as she grabbed an automatic machine gun, resembling an Uzi. In the midst of chaos, Lucas gained control of the vehicle and Lori skillfully handled the weapon. She quickly regained control of the steering wheel and whirled the car around. They were now positioned horizontally in the middle of the road. As the SUV was still converging upon them at a rapid speed, Lori continues firing. The shots hit the driver, causing him to lose control. Lori shoots the tires and the vehicle flipped over. She manages to fire one, last deadly shot at the SUV with the bloodsuckers trapped inside. Instantly, a massive explosion sends them into a fiery inferno, killing every vampire. She quickly turns the wheel and sped off.

"Are you alright?" Lori asked.

Lucas felt a sharp, throbbing pain in his head. He noticed blood running down his face, as his vision blurred and he began to lose consciousness.

"Is that a trick question or multiple choice?" He slurred sarcastically.

"Just hang on, Luc. I'm taking you to a safe place...I promise," Lori stated.

3

Silver Fangs

Lucas blacked out and his mind began drifting back to the horrors he witnessed as a child. Suddenly, the sound of gun shots in his dream awakened him. He found himself in a strange room lying on a bed and his head was bandaged. He could hear a loud argument downstairs. The entire Slade family was gathered in the study, as Nezera lashed out at her sister.

"Lo, your personal feelings have clouded your judgement, yet again. You've not only put yourself at risk, but the entire family. You're lucky to be alive!" Nez yelled.

"I didn't have time to abide by the rules of the road, Nez! I had very little time to react, so I improvised," Lori yelled back.

"Little sister, you're becoming far too reckless for me to ignore. Your antics are all over the news.

What if the authorities tracked your whereabouts?" Nezera asked angrily.

"Nez, that's enough. Your sister did what she had to do. We all know when decisions have to be made, things are hardly ever perfect," Nora explained.

"We were instructed to tread lightly, not attract attention! Now, because of her timeless infatuation with this reoccurring mortal, we're all at risk," Nezera shouted.

"Nezera, have you forgotten we're always at risk? This is no different than any other day. We have fought this war in the past," Joshua explained.

While eavesdropping, Lucas tiptoed down the steps. Instantly, each member of the family caught a whiff of his scent. He moved closer to the door trying to escape. Joshua quickly opened the door of the study and spotted Lucas trying to sneak out of the house.

"Lucas...I see you have awakened. Please join us. Everyone is very eager to meet you," Joshua said kindly.

Lucas felt awkward and very rude for trying to leave. However, he didn't know these people and he had no idea what they wanted from him. As he entered the study, he saw the entire family for the very first time.

"Welcome Lucas. I would like to formally introduce you to my family. Of course, you already know my daughter Lo and my wife Nora," Joshua said.

"Professor Grant?" Lucas inquired with amazement.

"Hello Lucas. Grant is my maiden name. I use it for protective reasons. My full name is Nora Grant Slade, but let that be our little secret. I'm sure you have many, many questions for us and I promise everything will become quite clear in a moment," she declared.

"Let me introduce you to the rest the family. This is Jeremiah and his wife Nezera. Nez is Lorelei's older sister," Joshua explained.

"It's nice to finally meet you, man," Jeremiah said as he shook Lucas's hand.

There was a slight twinge of hostility in Nezera's demeanor during the introduction. She was obviously annoyed by Lucas's presence.

"Last, but certainly not least, this is Alexander and his wife Abigail," Joshua stated.

"Hi Lucas, it's so nice meet you. Call me Abby, everyone else does," Abigail said with a smile. Each member of the Slade family looked extremely fit and well preserved. Not one hair out of place and not one wrinkle to be found.

Finally, getting to the matter at hand, Lucas wanted to know what the hell was going on.

"Can someone please tell me why I'm here?" Lucas asked.

As Joshua continued, you could hear a pin drop. "The reason you're here, Lucas, is for your own protection. This may be difficult to understand, however, it doesn't make it any less true. Try to keep an open mind when I tell you this. Amongst the shadows, meta-demonic evil exists. We live in a world where dark forces and nightmares are real. It's known as The United Blood Sovereign of Covens...The Vampire Consortium dating back to the dark ages."

"Vampires. You're kidding me, right?" Lucas said in disbelief.

"Lucas, I'm afraid tonight wasn't a dream. This is no practical joke and you're not imagining this," Lori explained.

"Bottom line Lucas, vampires do exist whether you choose to believe or not," Nora stated.

Lucas recalls the events of his earlier attack and the vague, unexplained occurrences of his childhood.

"The world is full of false notions, I'm afraid. The greatest trick the devil ever pulled was convincing man that he didn't exist. There are more of them than you realize. They exist in every city, state and country around the world. Vampires have existed amongst man for centuries," Joshua stated.

"How do you all know this?" Lucas asked.

Again, their expressions changed, as feelings of uneasiness crept back into the room.

"We hunt them, Lucas. Let's just say, we exist between worlds," Joshua proclaimed.

"What's that supposed to mean?" Lucas asked.

"It means, vampires are not the only Blood Immortals infecting others with the virus of their physiology. Every member of this family is neither all vampire nor all human, but an infusion of the two. Our kind is known by many names...Day-walkers, Dhampyres, Hybrids and Half-breeds. Officially, we are called Blood Sabers or Silver Fangs. We inherit strength, power, speed and the insatiable thirst for human blood from vampires. Lucas began to look even closer at each of them. Right away, he noticed the change in their eye color from black to gold. Before the room started to spin, Lucas noticed they were all sporting slightly overgrown teeth and visible platinum silver on their bottom canines. Nothing like the monsters he bared witness to earlier. The Slades were extremely beautiful and tamed creatures.

"Wow, I must say, that was an extremely wonderful, yet horrific presentation. Now, can someone please tell me what this has to do with me?" Lucas pleaded.

"Lucas, what do you remember about your parents...your father?" Nora asked.

"Very little, if anything, I'm afraid. I was barely five when my parents died," Lucas said.

"I knew your father very well. He was one of the leading pioneers of Arcane Science. He believed the infusion of magic and science could advance mankind on a genetic level. Your father's work involved the development of a bio-enchanted serum designed to enhance sections of the human genome. He was searching for ways to reprogram human genetic material, such as cellular re-growth, superior strength, agility, endurance, and healing. Your father was trying to improve the physiology of the human condition," Nora explained.

"You're talking about para-physical enhancement," Lucas stated.

"Yes, exactly," Nora replied.

"I thought the study of Alchemy was a myth, an urban legend. So, what happened?" Lucas asked.

"A stranger came calling one day, curious about your father's work. He offered your father his dream...a new lab, unlimited resources and all the money he would ever need to further his research. This stranger wanted to develop immunities to sunlight, silver and garlic. He commissioned your father to develop a cure for these frailties. He began customizing and enhancing chromosomes in the body, with hopes of creating genetically superior, blood immortals. Your father was so self-assured, that he tested the serum on himself. The enhancements made him immune to illness and disease. He also acquired superhuman capabilities, which altered his physiology. He called the serum "Night-worth," she explained.

"So, this stranger was a vampire?" Lucas asked.

"Yes, the blood immortal that's tracking you. His name is Dorian Ross and he is a very dangerous vampire. He runs a lowlife outfit called the "Dark Rogues". They're a bunch of fanatics obsessed with the advancement of the vampire species and conquering humanity.

"Ross had horrifying plans for humanity that your father refused to accept, so he and your mother tried to run. He realized he could never let Ross get his hands on those applications. So, he developed a failsafe, just in case he was killed and his work compromised," Nora stated.

"Lucas, did you ever wonder why you're so different? You've never caught a cold or broken a bone. You've never even lost a fight. The head injury you sustained earlier, has completely healed. Well, that's because you inherited "Night-worth" from your father. When he was killed and his blood went cold, the applications were destroyed and that's how he designed the cure. Ross needs you alive in order to harvest and extract the immunities from your blood," Joshua explained.

"Now, you know why your parents were murdered," Nora said.

"I only get fragments in the form of nightmares. I could never fully piece together, the events of that night," Lucas explained.

"Your grandfather had your memories of that horrific night erased. It is a chemical process, where latent memories slip through the cracks," Nora explained.

"Wow. Okay, okay...Vampires, Blood Sabers, Enhanced individuals...this is a lot to digest," Lucas said.

"Well, you don't have to take our word for it. There's someone who would like to have a word with you," Joshua said.

"I can't wait to hear this," Lucas said sarcastically. Joshua activated a holographic admitter, projecting a human-like, interactive projection of Lucas's father. Immediately, his doubts and disbeliefs were silenced. Without further delay, the man began speaking.

"Lucas, if you can view me as a projection, it means your mother and I have been dead for some time. Despite our attempts to keep you out of harm's way, we have failed. This is our last and final attempt to reach out to you from beyond. Son, I realize you don't know who to trust and you feel trapped in a nightmare of death and despair, but I promise, you are not alone. You will never be alone. If you are watching this, it also means you are amongst friends. Joshua, Nora, and the House of Slade have been my longtime allies. You can trust them. They can teach you about what you will soon face. As you have already discovered, the world is much darker, stranger, and far more dangerous place than you've realized. For the

longest time, I've searched for ways to improve the human condition. It was my life's work. Trying to rid humanity of diseases and evolve human physiology. This was during a time when I was naïve and would have done anything to fund my research. I trusted the wrong people and nearly brought the human race to the brink of destruction. Regardless of what you believe Luc, Vampires exist. They are a race far superior to that of humans. They possess no morality, compassion or remorse, and will not hesitate to kill or feed on the living, in order to achieve their own ends. Upon completing my research and experiments, I discovered why the United Blood Sovereign wanted to use my work. I had a moral responsibility to protect humanity from their capabilities. I took the treatments and injected them directly into my bloodstream and I gave Ross a defected cure to buy us time to escape. The treatments made me stronger, faster and more agile. Even then, I realized my research was not safe. I needed another foolproof failsafe. For years, your mother and I tried for a child, but were unsuccessful. However, everything changed when my genetic structure changed. You were born the next winter and my DNA was passed on to you. You might have noticed over the years, your scars, wounds and illnesses recover almost immediately. Your DNA is genetically engineered and far more complex than any human. You my son, are the key, the cure and the patriarch of a new era of mankind. Together, with the hybrid covens, you can bring about a new order of liberation for humanity. The legacy your mother and I risked our lives to preserve. Make no mistake, Dorian Ross is the most dangerous adversary we have ever faced. He is brilliant, sadistic and cruel. He will not hesitate to kill every single one of you. For the sake of humanity, he and those like him, must be destroyed. Lucas, your mother and I believe in you. You're not just anyone. You are the greatest accomplishment of our lives. My only regret is that I'm not there to see how you've blossomed. Always remember, we love you, son."

As the projection vanished, Lucas could see an expression of fear, as well as pride, on his father's face. The entire house was silent, as sadness and grief hit Lucas hard. Lori walked over and held his hand. She knew he needed comforting.

"Damn. I'm caught up in a real-life, fatal Vampire's Diary out this motherfucker!" Lucas stated.

"Well, at least his humor is still intact," Jeremiah said.

"I'm trying to understand... if they crave human blood and you crave human blood, what makes you all any different? If I'm the key to their evolution, why don't you just kill me and save yourselves the trouble?" Lucas asked.

"That's a fair question. There's no way to know whether you can trust us at all. But, I suspect your instincts and experience as a professional soldier, allows you to tell the difference between enemies and allies, Captain," Joshua said.

"We aren't monsters, Lucas. You should know the difference. If it were not for us risking our lives intervening on your behalf, Ross would have his claws into you by now," Nezera said.

"Nez, that's enough. Lucas has the right to ask questions. We have just dropped a huge bomb on him tonight," Nora said. She abruptly stormed out of the study. Jeremiah trailed behind Nez, with hopes of calming her down.

"Lucas never mind my sister. She's a bit emotional at times. We have nothing but the upmost respect for humanity and what the para-enhanced community calls "natural law". We're the only thing that stands between the vampires and your people. As for the thirst, the "Silver Fang" clan has taken the vow to not feed on humans and we can control our thirst," Lori claimed.

"It is our human nature that often places us in conflict with our predatory nature," Nora said.

"Well, what about the authorities?" Lucas asked.

"They own the police. They sink their claws into just about anything and anyone you could imagine…politics, finance and real-estate. They own over half of the globe. If we alert the cops, Ross and his men can track you," Joshua explained.

"Lucas, we want you to stay here with us," Nora suggested.

"I promise, you can trust us. There are no secrets and we don't bite...much," Lori said humorously.

"We will provide you with everything you need and you'll be well cared for," Nora said.

Meanwhile, on the other side of town, Dorian Ross and his team of vampires set up shop in an abandoned storage facility. The only surviving vampire from the pharmacy battle reported back to Ross.

"I remember sending eight of you, isn't that right?" Ross asked.

"He wasn't alone. He had a silver-fanged saber with him. She was highly trained and carried a silver, chained weapon with a blade at the end. She laid waste to them, as if they never existed," the henchman said.

Ross knew exactly who she was and who he was dealing with. He uttered one word, "Slade." He turned around, pointed a gun at his henchman's head, and pulled the trigger.

"Fail me again and next time the chamber won't be empty. Find out what local assets we have in the area. I want Shaw no matter what it takes. Without him, we have nothing," Ross said.

Judging by his immediate reaction, Ross was less than thrilled about the Slades. He knew they were a formidable force to be reckoned with. He began contemplating his next move against the Slades and how he would lure them long enough to get to his target.

4

Birth of the Blood Immortals

Back at the Slade family home, Lucas made good on his decision to stay under their protection. Lori also kept her promise to answer any questions Lucas might have. First and foremost, she revealed the seller where they keep cloned animal blood. This is where we learn to control and quench our thirst. Afterwards, Lori took Lucas to her bedroom and they spent all night talking. As Lucas asked questions, Lori gladly answered. Although he knew it was improper to ask a woman her age, his curiosity got the best of him.

"This has been my life for nearly two hundred years. We Sabers, are identical to our predecessors in almost every way, except we are immune to sunlight, metallic silver, and even garlic. Like the vampires, we can pass on the physiology of our species through a single bite," Lori explained.

"So, how did the Saber strain arise?" Lucas asked.

Lori went downstairs and came back with a huge book. She referred to it as the "Sanguinoso Noctemos", the text of the blood elders. The book was very thick and ancient and its pages were worn and aged. She blew off the dust and opened the book to the first page.

"The birth of vampirism originated during the Dark Ages in Central Romania from House Vandran. Lord Codrin had two sons, Darius and Marius. Darius was the oldest and would inherit the Kingdom upon his father's death. Marius was jealous of his brother's future inheritance. He understood power is not bestowed nor given, it's taken. So, he sought the dark powers of the Dracul. They were hideous, fanged demons who dwelled amongst the darkness of the Mortem Caves deep within the mountains. Standing before the Dracul Queen and her hive, Marius demanded the power to overthrow his father and brother, in order to seize the throne for himself. The Dracul Queen gives Marius her blood, turning him into the first blood immortal…a vampire. He can only exist in darkness and has an unquenchable thirst for blood. Marius returns to the Kingdom and viciously usurps the

throne by murdering his father and brother, thus crowning himself King. Promising his people immortality, the Kingdom quickly turned into a city of the undead. He would become known as **Lord Marius** Vladimir **Vandran**. As Marius's cruelty grew, so did his ambition for power…one feeding the other. Many years later, he envisioned a plan to conquer and annihilate his enemies throughout the country of Romania. Recognizing his vulnerability to sunlight, he and his legions of the undead could not set foot on the battlefield during the day. He needed soldiers, assassins and mercenaries who possessed similar supernatural abilities to exist in the daylight. Utilizing the ancient trade routes out of Africa, India and even Asia, he began importing female slaves into central Romania. During the night, he and his generals raped and infected these young women, breeding a whole new race of immortal slaves capable of walking in the daylight. Many of these young women perished while giving birth to the infant creatures.

Every child was taken, whipped, enslaved and trained in the combative arts by Vandran's Imperial Guard. These children grew to desire the same insatiable thirst for blood and possessed the same strength, speed and agility of a vampire. These child *soldiers grew faster than any human and immediately reached adulthood within a few years of being born. Marius dispatched his* Blood *Sabers to obliterate every kingdom, village, town and region who opposed his rule. With the strength and speed of a Saber, one could solely lay waste to an entire army in one day.*

Vandran ruled for two hundred years, due to the vicious customs. His ambition eventually grew to conquering all of Europe. Eventually, his fearmongering and dismay for the species he created, caused him to order the eradication of the Saber strain. He feared them because they could possibly threaten his rule. It was known that Sabers were more powerful than Vampires, given the physiology of their strain. Quite naturally, every Blood *Saber began to rebel. They demanded freedom, as they turned their gifts and abilities onto their predecessors, laying waste to Vandran's entire Kingdom. Years later, in dwindling numbers, we established their own consortium and hierarchy. The hierarchy is composed of three royal houses, the Gold-fangs, the Silver-fangs, and the Iron-fangs. We constructed our network and society living amongst the mortals in shadow-protecting and observing,"* Lori explained.

"What became of the king?" Lucas asked.

"No one really knows. Some say Vandran was killed during the Saber's rebellion. Others suspect he was imprisoned in a metal coffin and buried deep below ground in an underwater cave. The ones that know for sure, have taken a blood-oath to never speak of those final days of the rebellion or discuss the events of Vandran's demise. One of the Saber Lords, who is old enough to remember the days of the rebellion, lives in this very house," Lori said.

"Joshua is a Silver-fang? He's one of the high-born Saber Lords that still lives? He's over six hundred years old?" Lucas inquired.

"Now, that you understand why this blood feud exists and why we stand with humanity, do me one favor...don't ever raise that question to Joshua or anyone in this house, for that matter," Lori sternly advised.

"So, where do you fit into all of this?" Lucas asked.

"Many years ago, my sister and I were in a bind and Joshua came and offered us a chance at another life," Lori concluded.

"Yeah, but that's not all there is, is there?" Lucas asked.

"Stick around, if you want me to divulge more of my secrets, Captain," she said.

"I noticed the ink on your shoulders, back and arms. All of you have tribal markings on your bodies. What does it symbolize?" Lucas asked.

"These are the tribal glyphs of our house, our coven...taken from the Sanguinoso Noctemos. They are the Mark of the Saber," she stated, locating the symbols in the book.

They talked for hours upon hours. Finally, Lucas fell asleep with Lori in his arms. As she watched Lucas sleep, she felt so much joy and admiration. She knew, at that very moment, Lucas was the one. Lori felt highly protective of him and would give her life to secure his safety. However, she wasn't ready to tell him he's the reincarnated look-a-like she once loved...a reoccurrence in time.

In the days to come, Lucas and Lori were attached at the hip. She accompanied him throughout campus and sat with him during his classes. She became his personal bodyguard. Even during his workouts and training, she was right by his side.

Lori's cell phone rang while they were in the park. It was Joshua.

"Lo, I need you to bring Lucas home. The Colonel has just arrived." Joshua insisted.

Lori and Lucas quickly left the park. She made him aware that his grandfather was at the house. Lucas felt disheartened, knowing the truth had been withheld from him.

Joshua and the Colonel waited patiently for Lucas and Lori's return. They entered into a deep discussion about what was revealed to his grandson. The Colonel expressed his disapproval of their decision to show Lucas the holographic recording.

"He's been through enough trauma," the Colonel stated.

"Protection from the truth was relevant when Lucas was a boy. Now, he's a young man who deserves to know the mystery that's been haunting him his entire life...and is still haunting him," Nora replied.

"He is being hunted by the same bloodsucker that murdered his parents and he needs to be prepared to fight for his survival," Joshua said.

"Yes, I know. Saving humanity rests on his shoulders. Damn, I was hoping this day would never come," the Colonel said.

"We can protect him and care for him. He doesn't have to bare this burden alone," Joshua said.

Nora agreed with her husband. Lucas was in great hands and would be protected, even from the darker sides of themselves.

"Josh, do you still think about that night?" The Colonel asked.

"I have lived many lifetimes and bared witness to many atrocities over the centuries, but the horrible events of that night plague my mind more than anything. The horrific murder of my friends was despicable and unforgivable," Joshua stated.

"Sadly, it was too late to save my son and daughter-in law. But, I'll never forget the look in my grandson's eyes when I found him. Remember? He hid in that underground tunnel for two days. I knew the moment we brought him out, he would never be the same innocent, little boy," the Colonel exclaimed.

"This is not your burden to bear alone. We were both trying to save the people we cared about that night, but it was too late, Colonel," Joshua reassured.

Lucas and Lori finally arrived and Lucas did not break stride getting out of the car. He was eager to have words with his grandfather. Before the Colonel could utter a single word, Lucas yelled out of frustration, "Old man, you could have told me what the nightmares meant, instead of letting me think I was insane for the last eighteen years. You had no right to do what you did!" Lucas shouted.

"Luc, I know. I did what I thought was best for you at that time. I didn't want you tormented with a life of horrors. I did what I had to do to protect you," the Colonel explained.

"What you did...changed nothing! My life is still filled with horrors and demons that I can't bury. It would have been better to hear the truth from you," Lucas exclaimed.

As Lucas confronted his grandfather, Lori stood quietly by Nora's side witnessing her love's disappointment.

"So, is this what it was all about...the training, living on military bases, and constantly moving from place to place?" Lucas asked.

The Colonel's response was a simple nod.

"Ross is determined to get what your father stored in your DNA. The bastard wants to trigger some damn Vampire Armageddon," the Colonel explained. Lucas began thinking back on his life on the military bases with his grandfather. During combat training, he always seemed naturally superior in strength and agility. He was always the last one standing, no matter how great the odds.

"Oh yeah, and my blood...I'm a para-enhanced individual, too huh? This explains why I could toss a ball the entire length of a football field and single-handedly undermine entire squadrons of men. I was always the last man standing without a fucking scratch...not one fucking scratch. I'm on information overload. Before yesterday, I didn't even know vampires existed and now, I'm being hunted by them.

Not to mention, I could also be responsible for the destruction of humanity. That is, if Ross and his blood-ghoul cronies get their hands on me. No pressure, though," Lucas declared sarcastically.

"So, what happens now? How do I kill this bastard?" Lucas asked.

"Well, you have two choices, Luc. You can continue being schooled under the protection of the Silver-fang clan and learn what it takes to kill one of these cold-blood bastards or you can come with me. It's entirely up to you," the Colonel explained.

Lucas gazed at Lori and she gazed back, as if she already his answer.

"Well, I am tired of running from an unknown past, with no escape. It's time to face my most horrible nightmares," Lucas said.

"Hunting and killing vampires just so happens to be our specialty Mr. Shaw...or should I say, Captain. As superior as you may be, you still lack the blood-strength and durability that's necessary to defeat a vampire. The strength of a blood immortal increases over time," Joshua explained.

"So, how do I complete my mission and live to fight another day?" Lucas asked.

"Your training begins tomorrow, so get a good night's sleep...you'll need it," Joshua replied.

"Promise me, you will protect my grandson...even from yourselves," The Colonel pleaded.

"We understand you may have reservations about Lucas living with a bunch of half-breed bloodsuckers, but we're sworn to oath to not feed on human flesh. We obey natural law and it's non-negotiable. Lucas will be cared for and well protected," Nora explained.

Although the Slades are the beacons of righteousness and the defenders of humanity, the Colonel was still not convinced of their intentions. He noticed Lucas was extremely cozy with the pretty Saber as they walked in.

The Colonel accepted his grandson's decision to stay under their protection of and to confront Ross. As he prepared to leave, he requested a few minutes with his grandson.

"Luc, you are the only family I have left, so watch your back. I know their hearts are in the right place, but the Slades are still half-human. Your father trusted them and they will train you to kill those blood-thirsty bastards. That being said, they still hunger for the taste of human blood. Please stay focused because I can see you're quite smitten with little Ms. Huntress over there," the Colonel teased.

"Granddaddy, I'll be fine. If they wanted to kill me, they would have done so by now. My main goal is to survive this asshole, Ross," Lucas said.

"Alright son, I'm going to let you make the call. If you ever need me, you know how to reach me," the Colonel stated.

He left Lucas to make his own decisions, as he pulled out of the driveway. The Colonel wasn't one for mincing words when it came to his family. As Lucas entered the house, Joshua was waiting.

"Shall we begin, Captain?" He asked.

"Sure, let's get this show on the road," Lucas responded.

Joshua began lecturing, "Hunting vampires is notoriously difficult to accomplish, Lucas. Their physiology is highly resilient, making it easy for them to recover instantly. Feeding on human blood enhances their blood-strength and allows them to maintain their para-physical capabilities, such as their resistance to injury, pain, and recovery. They also have superior strength, speed and agility, as well as, the ability to render themselves invisible."

5

Training a Human Hunter

Strolling down to the lower level of house, Lucas noticed the basement was extremely high-tech. There were stainless-steel, automatic, storage drawers containing an arsenal of weaponry. They had everything from automatic rifles, handguns and bullets, to throwing projectiles, a limitless collection of blades, swords, and machetes. It was like nothing Lucas had ever seen. The Slade's technology, resources and weaponry was advanced decades beyond the modern world.

Joshua continued his lecture on how to exploit a vampire's weaknesses. "Vampires are severely allergic to silver, garlic and ultraviolet radiation. As in every mythology and legend of vampires, direct sunlight incinerates their flesh, reducing them to charred corpses. Silver has always been the ultimate weapon against the cursed and the damned, since the betrayal of Jesus Christ," he explained.

"It is easier for a Saber to destroy a vampire, simply because their blood, strength and physiologies are very similar. We possess the same superior strength, speed, agility and regenerative capabilities as they do," Joshua stated. As they concluded the lecture and tour of the armory, Lucas began familiarizing himself with the bladed weapons. He selected a machete, a medium-to-close range weapon, capable of devastating attacks and killing blows at the hands of its wielder. The soldier in him began toying with the rifles and handguns.

"Not a bad selection of ordinance. I see, you favor the Filipino System of combat," Joshua stated.

"Yes, I do. I'm damn-near surgical when utilizing a blade. The old man had me research and train in every system of combat known to man," Lucas boasted.

"Excellent, now get some rest. Tomorrow, I want to see your skills," Joshua insisted.

Lucas turned his attention to a half-covered painting in the corner of the storage area.

"What's this?" He asked.

"Oh, I wouldn't touch that, if I were you. That portrait is extremely personal to Lo and it's completely off limits to everyone in this house," Joshua proclaimed.

"Well, if that's the case, why is it in the open?" Lucas asked.

Before Joshua could answer, Lori appeared and said, "Good question. Perhaps, I should move it. You're very intuitive for a man who's stumbled his way into a shit storm."

"Well, I guess I should have known. You guys are not without your secrets," Lucas mumbled under his breath.

"Everyone has their secrets, Captain. You'll have to put in valuable time to learn mine," Lori flirted.

As Joshua and Lucas left the basement, Lori stayed behind. She removed the sheet from the painting and stared at her prized possession. As she gazed, her eyes changed colors. It was obvious she had an intimate connection to the portrait. She gently placed the sheet back over it and moved it out of sight.

Suddenly, Nora appeared behind her and asked, "So, I'm assuming you haven't told him?"

"No, not yet. I'm not ready and I'm terrified of how he'll react, if he sees it. It's happening just as predicted and I can feel myself falling all over again. I'm drawn to him and I can't fight the feeling. I can't lose him this time, but nature will have to run its course. All of these years, I've had to remain strong and cold-hearted to survive this infinite life. Now, I can actually feel my heartbeat again. I feel totally unmade. It's very difficult knowing what it's like to feel again...to have emotions," Lori expressed.

"Lo, it's perfectly fine to succumb to your feelings. After all, we are half-human. I have always known your heart, even though you've kept it distant. You deserve to experience what the rest of us share every night. A true love that is beautiful and long-lasting. You have nothing to be ashamed of," Nora reassured.

She embraced Lori with a motherly hug and said, "We all love you and want the absolute best for you."

"Thanks Nora," Lori replied.

The next morning, Lucas trained in an abandoned storage property the Slades owned. Although his body was well conditioned due to his military training and physical enhancements, he still lacked the abilities to combat vampires. For numerous days, Joshua put Lucas through rigorous and intense training. Molding his body into a lethal, sculpted fighting machine. At times, Lucas would return to the Slade's home, barely capable of standing. Night after night, Lori would have the pleasure of massaging and nursing his body back to health for the next session.

One afternoon, Lucas squared off against Joshua in the family's Lagoon-style pond. Testing Lucas's close-quarter, combative prowess, Joshua identified certain weaknesses. The technique boosted Lucas's awareness while combating a blood- immortal. Everyone gathered around bearing witness to Lucas attempting to overcome Joshua's overwhelming speed and strength. He continued to evade and avoid Lucas's every attempt to strike him, even taking some of Lucas's blows with little to no ill-effect. Joshua executed Saber-strain reflexes, fighting skills and abilities that could not be matched. The Slades could see that Lucas displayed heart and courage as he fought, gaining their respect. They recognized he was special. Joshua struck Lucas with an overwhelming blow, dropping him to his knees. Lori watched intensely from her balcony. After the brutal lesson, the family made their way back into the house. Alexander and Jeremiah lifted Lucas to his feet. He was covered in blood and sweat. Joshua sat close by, recovering his breathing.

"The world is full of false notions, Captain. Rest assured, you're dealing with something your military experience has never shown you. Vampires do not move like ordinary humans. The elasticity of a blood-immortal is enhanced to inhuman levels. This allows their movements to be highly erratic at high speeds, making them almost impossible to track. They also possess the ability to adhere to surfaces unaided. Your average blood-immortal can survive a drop from a ten-story building, landing without injury or harm. We have a long way to go," Joshua explained.

"There aren't many that can hold their own against Joshua. Not even most Sabers," Jeremiah said.

"Yeah, I can feel that," Lucas replied.

"Joshua is one of the first and oldest Saber Lords. He's also among the strongest of our race," Jeremiah explained.

Lori suddenly came down the steps with bandages, alcohol and other first-aid supplies. Lucas had never experienced defeat. His minor bruises and cuts didn't affect him as much as his ego. Lori grabbed Lucas by the hand and led him upstairs to her suite. She tended to his cuts as they quickly began to heal on their own.

"Wow, you heal almost instantly, as we do...that's extraordinary," Lori gleamed.

"You have courage and you are a great fighter, but you must remove your ego from the equation," Lori explained.

"Why haven't I seen you all bleed? I got in some good shots down there and Joshua doesn't have a bruise or cut to show for it. Why is that?" Lucas asked.

"As you already know, Joshua is one of the first of the Saber Lords. He's an elder of the Hybrid race. A Saber's strength and para-physical abilities increase with age. The longer we live, the stronger we become.

This extraordinary healing factor makes it hard for us to be killed. It is also responsible for prolonging our lifespan by thousands of years," Lori explained.

She took a small pocketknife and cut the middle of her forearm. Immediately, the blood started to stream from her wound and suddenly the wound healed, disappearing instantly. Lucas could hardly believe his eyes. He was totally amazed.

"So, why the name Killcount? What's the story?" Lori asked.

"Isn't it obvious?" Lucas replied.

"Oh yes, it's very obvious, but I want to hear your version, Captain." Lori said.

"Ambush operations and demolition was my specialty and after a five-year tour in Jakarta, I joined a Shadow-ops Think-tank Unit to take down rogue militias and regimes all over the world. I racked up a sizable body count of over 645 confirmed kills. Government agencies and the military started calling me Killcount. They would send me to designated jungles and villages alone. I would lace the entire environment with triggered explosives, tripwires, land mines and death traps. Those regimes didn't even know what hit them. The men my traps couldn't kill, I killed. I was extremely efficient...in and out without a scratch, not one fucking scratch," Lucas described.

"Seems like you were the best at what you did. Why did you leave?" Lori asked.

"I lost my desire for it...the constant killing. There was always another target and rogue regime to conquer. I could no longer distinguish the heroes from the villains. The righteous and the wicked were all intertwined and I wanted another life for myself. When my time comes to face my Lord God on Judgement day, I want to do it with my head held high," Lucas explained.

Without a moment's notice, their eyes locked and she grabbed the back of his head, pulling him closely for a kiss. Quickly, they began to undress, as their hunger for one another was building, uncontrollably.

Lucas removed Lori's tank top, revealing her exquisite, voluptuous breasts. He applied succulent kisses to her nipples as he gently caressed and cupped them in the palms of his hands. Feeling an instant state of euphoria, Lori moaned with desire. He removed her jeans, revealing her beautiful thighs and black, lace panties. As he gazed up at her, Lori's irises became golden and her platinum fangs began to enlarge. At first, she hesitated, thinking Lucas would be horrified by her fierce, animalistic features. Instead, he pulled her closer and said, "You are the most alluring creature I've ever seen."

"Is this better, knowing exactly who I am?" she asked.

"I'm not one to judge, babe. My feelings for you are real. Something I've never felt before," Lucas whispered.

She knew the exact connection they shared, although she still wasn't ready to divulge the truth of her past. They continued to undress each other down to their bare bodies. Lucas couldn't help but stare at Lori's magnificent figure, as they continued kissing.

"Come with me," she said, leading him to the shower.

He posted her body up against the shower glass with her legs spread wide open. As Lucas entered inside her, she pulled him into her body and they kissed deeply. Lust, steam and heat filled the shower as they made passionate love. Soaked and wet, he continued to stroke her body in every way, as her orgasms grew more intense. Lori could barely contain herself. She moaned loudly, as she climaxed over and over. With excitement, Lucas gazed into her beautiful amber-colored eyes. Lori managed to control her thirst with every intimate encounter. It was no easy feat, while resisting the urge to feast on his flesh. She could never hurt or lay a hand on him. He was more precious than life itself.

Lori rapped her arms around Lucas's hard body and held him close as he reached his peak, collapsing in her arms. For a moment, they stared deep into each other's eyes as the water and steam engulfed their bodies.

"Finally, I have found you, Captain," she whispered.

As they stepped out of the shower, Lucas grabbed a soft, black towel to dry Lori's body. She displayed weakness and vulnerability, resembling a young girl being cuddled for the first time.

Entering her bedroom, she removed the towel and jumped back into Lucas's arms, wrapping her legs around his waist. They continued to kiss their way to the bed and she landing directly on top of him. It was apparent that Lori was hungry for yet, another round. With his head between her legs, Lucas enjoyed licking, sucking, and kissing her clit. Tasting the intensity of every orgasm her body produced. While tugging on her soft bush, he caused her eyes to roll back. For her, it was like having a second G-spot. Lori noticed Lucas was rock hard, so she placed him back inside of her and rode him into ecstasy. Meanwhile, in the room down the hall, Nezera was not particularly thrilled about Lucas and Lori hooking up, as she explained her reservations to Jeremiah.

"Nez, let her be. She's come a long way and she knows what she's doing. Besides, this is the most emotion we've seen in centuries," Jeremiah explained.

"No one knows my sister like I do. She will carelessly risk it all for him, just like she did before. Sadly, we will all be affected by her choices this time," Nezera stated with dismay.

"Honey, isn't that what love is, risking everything for the one you love, even if it's lifetime after lifetime? You can't expect her to roam from centuries as an empty shell. Babe, sometimes you just need to take a step back and let God do the work," Jeremiah answered.

"Re-occurrences...can this world get any stranger?" Nezera asked.

"Look at us. We've all lived well beyond our time, just like many other anomalies of this world," Jeremiah declared.

As the night was winding down, Lori stayed awake after a second round of sweet lovemaking. Lucas was fast asleep. As she got out of bed, Lori wrapped herself in the towel and made her way back to the shower. As the water poured down on her face, Lori reminisced back to the year 1787, when the man she once loved begged her to escape with him.

"Lorelei, we can have the life we've always dreamed of. We can escape to a more enlightened part of this country and live our lives beyond the confinements of this plantation. Please take a chance with me," he pleaded.

As Lori reflected back in time, her tears mixed with the water and steam of the shower. She felt blessed to have been given a second chance with the man she loved, even if he was a more modern-day version of himself. The next morning, Lucas awakened and began preparing for more of Joshua's grueling training. He followed Joshua and Lori into the forest where a cache of weaponry was positioned on a long table. There were wooden stakes, daggers, tomahawks, swords, short spears, machetes and other exotic blades used to kill vampires.

"You must know your weapons, just as a carpenter must know his tools. It's simply not enough to just pull a trigger," Lori advised.

"Let's get to work Lucas," Joshua said.

Lucas observed the forest in the back of the Slade's home. It was an elaborate training ground and obstacle course, which they designed. There were countless targets on the trees. Lori took one of the wooden stakes and launched it into the middle of the target, without a second look. Her aim was very precise, indeed. She also demonstrated her skills by whipping her chained weapon. At will, she could manifest her weapon out of thin air and into the palms of her hands, while shattering the pottery hanging high among the trees. The Silver Fangs aka House of Slade possessed a mystical ability of weapon manifestation. They described it as necro-conjuring, a voodoo-craft that only high-born Blood Sabers could perform to dispatch their enemies. Lori's secondary weapon was the Samurai sword. She could wield it at above-average speed, accuracy and precision. Her form while using the weapons, was impeccable. It was obvious she was designed to kill vampires. Lucas was beyond impressed and somewhat aroused by her display of skill. Lori possessed a special uniqueness her own kind could only dream of.

Joshua also moved with a certain fluidity and grace, as if the weapons were an extension of his body. It was clear Lucas did not possess the same level of fluidity and grace. His form with many of the weapons was somewhat choppy and uncoordinated.

"Start at about forty-percent. Do not overextend your reach and slashing motions. Speed equals death, so allow yourself to blend with the weapons you wield. Only then, will your form and movements become faster and unstoppable," Joshua explained.

"You do realize, I have trained in close-quarter combat," Lucas stated.

"No Captain. Not like this, you haven't," he warned.

6

Duels and Dinner

Day after day, weapon after weapon, Joshua's words and combat philosophies became somewhat mundane, but it carried purpose and great value. He was many things to the Slade family. The family patriarch and mentor, the "Silver Fang" Saber, as well as, the headhunter and combat instructor.

As time passed, Lucas sparred against every member of the family. Each one was an experienced Hunter, specializing in the use of their own customized weaponry. Nezera, however, was not very fond of Lucas. As the sun began set, tracking and evasion was the next lesson. The object of the exercise was to track Nezera throughout the woods. Keeping up with her was physically impossible for Luc, given her speed and agility. She could leap from tree to tree with ease and flank Lucas in merely a half-a-second. Nezera taunted Lucas, while attempting to draw on this frustrations and emotions. She could glide past him, knock him to the ground and toss him in the air many times over. In turn, Lucas and Lori created a hologram module to fool Nezera. His skills improved greatly. Also, his fluidity and grace with each weapon developed tremendously. Sparring hand-to-hand with Joshua and Lori was no easy feat. It was nearly impossible for Lucas to overcome. They truly possessed para-physical abilities no ordinary human could match. Their speed, strength, agility, and movements matched that of a blood immortal. Each and every night, Lucas suffered intense wounds. However, due to his accelerated healing, his injuries recovered overnight.

"Speed you will not possess. Strength you will not possess. Your enemies have the ability to render themselves invisible to the human eye. At times, you won't be able to depend on your own sight. Only wits, senses, and the ability to perceive and predict will save you. You have to attack where your opponent is going to be, not where he is. Perceive and predict, but do not anticipate," Joshua professed.

He placed a dark blindfold over Lucas's eyes and said, "In order to be a beacon of light, you must first journey through the darkness. Starting now, you will train without the most dominant of senses...your sight."

"This should be interesting. I have never fucked a man in blindfold before. Oh well, there is a first time for everything," Lori whispered in Luc's ear.

During the first couple of days, Lucas was totally out of his element, when training while blindfolded. As he sparred against Joshua, Lori, Jeremiah, Alexander, and Nora, he realized fighting blind was gravely challenging.

Joshua taunted Lucas stating, "No engagement of combat is ever fair."

One by one, they struck Lucas until they laid him out in the Lagoon. As the training became more intense, so did his injuries. Many nights, he would return with his face and body in dripping. The Slades sensed and smelled the blood emanating from Lucas's body. Each of them managed to keep distance, while controlling the hunger lurking inside. Although, Lucas was highly proficient in automatic weaponry, Joshua decided to train him in response time and coordination.

He instructed Lucas to track the targets, reiterating how vampires move erratically and incredibly fast.

On the last day of training, Joshua blindfolded Lucas. The family surrounded them in the Lagoon.

"Choose your weapon!" Joshua demanded.

Lucas grabbed a short spear and a Machete-Saber sword. He could hear the water rippling under their feet. As the training session became more intense, Luc's enhanced skills began to manifest, as he outmaneuvered each of his attackers. He used both the spear and saber, as if they were extensions of himself. All the while, his confidence magnified, as his fear of darkness disappeared.

He could hear the sound of a metal chain rattling and he knew it was her. Lori often used her modified, chained Kyoketsu Shoge to strike from long distances. It's a particularly hard weapon to handle, even in the hands of a Master, such as Lori. Like the rest of her family, she's had centuries to perfect the weapon. Lucas was at an incredible disadvantage. While adding insult to injury, he was fighting a master Saber-Siren blindfolded. Lori was eager to test his newfound abilities, as she stepped into the water of the Lagoon.

She truly didn't want to injure Lucas, but she also had cruel intentions as they began to spar. She knew this exercise would only make him stronger and more resilient.

"Are you ready?" She asked.

"As ready as I will ever be. Let's get it!" Lucas shouted.

She tossed the chain with the blade flying towards Lucas. He swiftly hit it away from his face, utilizing his Saber sword. Lori then retracted the chain and tossed it. The weapon bounced off the water and pounded Lucas's right leg. The chain began to wrap tightly around Lucas's leg. She tugged, causing him to corkscrew in mid-air and splash into the water. He landed hard on his back. He began moaning in pain, while mustering the strength to rise to his feet. Lucas retrieved his weapons and positioned in a combative stance. He turned his head to the side to utilize his hearing and track her movements. Lori wrapped the chain around her body and used the dagger to cut and deflect. She swiped at Lucas, drawing on his lack of focus and balance, as he swung at the air.

"Learn to see with more than your eyes. Except your fear of the unknown and embrace it," Joshua instructed. Their weapons clashed as they continued to swing violently at one another.

Lori tagged Lucas with a fierce sweep. Yet again, he managed to recover. As he continued to track the sounds of her movements, he evaded her attacks completely and gained a sizable advantage, which put her on the defensive. The rest of the family was stunned to see Lucas take lead over Lori's incredible abilities. His combative flow increased as his movements and form became crisper and more efficient. It was as if he could feel and predict Lori's every movement. He completed the challenge with a magnificent stroke, timed perfectly and executed precisely. Lori was pleasantly surprised by his vigor. She smiled at him and said, "Wow, I must say...I'm very impressed."

The entire family began applauding with excitement. "Impressive indeed," Joshua said, as he walked over to them. He was filled with joy knowing he had produced, yet another, great Hunter. Joshua presented Lucas with a new, customized Samurai Katana sword, as a reward.

"Remember Lucas, your true strength is not what lies in your muscles and your fists...they are merely a delivery system for what resides in your heart and soul," Joshua explained.

"I've heard that many times before," Lucas sadly stated.

"I know. Your father expressed those exact sentiments to you as a child. And like your father, I trust what exists in here," Joshua stated, pointing at Lucas's chest.

Although Joshua was an intimidating badass, he was also incredibly spiritual. He deeply believed in the spiritual world, but how could he not? Vampires and Sabers were not the only para-enhanced species. There were many para-natural species in existence, but they managed to fly under the radar.

As the sun began to set, Lori decided to host a surprise dinner for Lucas. As he cleaned up and got dressed, she was downstairs in the kitchen with Nora and Abigail preparing a fancy meal for her dude. As they were cooking, Nezera entered the kitchen.

"So, here we are going above and beyond for this mortal. Damn, the power of the dingus has your mind all twisted up...again. I certainly hope things end up a lot better than last time," Nez quipped. Lori ignored her sister and continued seasoning and marinating the food.

"Nez, stop antagonizing her. You're still fighting against your sister's happiness," Nora stated.

"If it were anyone else, she would have my blessing, hands down. But, not him. I'm anticipating the day when things will come back to wreak havoc on this house," Nez said angrily.

She turned to Lori and stated, "Does he know about the history between the two of you? Does he know he's a reoccurrence and you were in love with his forefather...his reincarnated carbon-copy? So, I am guessing you haven't shown him the painting you keep locked away in the basement."

Lori's temper began to flare, as she stabbed the wooden counter with the knife she used to dice the food. As her agitation grew, her irises turned golden.

"I will tell him when I'm damn good and ready...not one second before. Now, if you will excuse me, I have a date," Lori said.

She politely excused herself from the kitchen and went upstairs to pick out the magnificent red and black, laced dress from her closet. Her goal was to entice Lucas in every way possible. The dress was a perfect combination of elegance and sexy. She was laying it on her bed, when she suddenly noticed Abigail standing at the door.

"Are you alright?" Abigail asked as she entered the room.

"Yeah, I'm fine. Why?" Lori asked.

"I realize Nez was stirring up old wounds and I know it struck a chord," Abigail consoled.

"Abby, I've gotten used to Nez's overbearing attitude. She can be very obnoxious and protective. Please know, she's the least of my worries," Lori replied, in a cavalier tone.

Abigail didn't push the issue. She shook her head and changed the subject, as her attention was drawn to the fabulous, stiletto heels in Lori's closet.

"You know, those heels go perfectly with that dress, girl. But seriously, you have to let me do something with that thick hair of yours," Abigail said.

"Alright, just let me jump in the shower," Lori giggled.

Abigail pulled out the heels and waited patiently in Lori's room. She even picked out some jewelry Lori hadn't worn in years. She chose a dazzling, 3-carat diamond necklace, with earrings to match. Meanwhile, as Lucas arrived downstairs, looking extremely dapper, Jeremiah and Alexander slyly prevented him from entering the kitchen or Lori's room. They agreed to keep him occupied, as not to spoil the surprise.

"So Luc, I know you still have some unanswered questions. But first allow us to apologize for beating your ass these last few weeks," Jeremiah said.

"Well yeah...no need to apologize. I'm actually very grateful," Lucas replied.

"Okay then, ask away my brother," Jeremiah said.

"Is everyone in this house booed-up?" Lucas asked.

"Things can't get any more obvious than that, with the exception of you know who. Lo is unique, an acquired taste for some," Jeremiah explained.

"Lori?" Lucas asked.

"Yes…she was born Lorelei Angelica Brown. After she became a Saber Siren, she shortened her name to Lori Slade. She has always shielded herself from romance and attachment, at least until now. I never thought I would see the day when she would fall for a mortal man. Then again, you're not just any mortal, are you?" Jeremiah asked.

"Lori has always carried, within her, the mystique of an untouchable huntress," Alexander explained.

"So, were you all turned by Joshua?" Lucas asked.

"Yes, we all owe our freedom and immortality to him. You see, we all lived during an era where people of color were owned and enslaved in some fashion or another. We were considered to be property and pieces of meat. Since then, we have lived many different lives and bared witness to many evils of the world. Joshua is a liberator and savior in many ways. He came along and freed each of us from our own personal demons, in exchange for living with only one…the thirst. He offered us new lives. We were all dangling between life and death. He could offer the same to you, if you so choose," Jeremiah explained.

"So, how does it feel to be dating an older woman?" He asked.

"What do you mean? Please explain," Lucas inquired.

"Do you realize how old we are? We age once every millennia, but it's our incredible, regenerative healing factor and DNA that causes us to age at a much slower rate than humans. You see, after a while you kind of lose track of the number and it becomes less important," Jeremiah explained.

"Days turn into weeks, weeks into months, and months into years....years into centuries and beyond. For us this process operates at hyper-speed. This is the trick of immortality. Days bleed together and really, if it wasn't for my technological-focused wifey, we wouldn't even know the time," Alexander said smiling at Abigail.

"You see, the world changes, but we don't. That's what makes immortality such a burden for those who don't have someone to share it with," Jeremiah said.

As Jeremiah and Alexander explained the concept of age and immortality, Lucas was amazed at how long they've lived, but remained so youthful. None of them appeared to be a day over twenty years old.

The fellas continued to bond, as Abigail styled Lori's hair into a beautiful, halo braid, which she adorned with gold accessories.

"Do you plan to turn him?" Abigail asked.

"Uhhh boundaries...you always did love pushing my limits, Abby. Possibly, but that's his choice to make. It's not up to me or anyone else, but especially me. I'm still willing to love him regardless, even if only for a little while," she explained.

"Wow, that doesn't sound like the Lorelei Slade I know, with her rules and no attachments. We've never seen you this way, although I must say, I do enjoy your softer, more sensitive side. I've always known you were a true romantic at heart," Abigail teased.

"Why is everyone so concerned with my rules?" Lori asked. "We just want what's best for you, Lo. We're family and we'll always be concerned. I thought you would've figured that out by now, Siren," Abigail said.

"I love you too, sis," Lori beamed.

As she finished Lori's hair, Abby smiled and said, "It's refreshing to see the corners of your mouth actually turn up. I took the liberty of picking out some jewelry for you to wear tonight.

"Okay Abby, you're going a little overboard here. Bling is not really my thing," Lori said.

"No, this is exactly what's needed. You've been in the Siren-zone so long, you've forgotten how to be a lady...that's where I come in. I do realize you've given Lucas the business and quite well, I might add, but you also want a man to find you irresistible with your clothes on," Abigail said playfully.

7

Night Out with a Siren

ownstairs, as Lucas and the boys wrapped up their conversation, Lori stepped in the doorway looking absolutely gorgeous. Immediately, their eyes opened wide with amazement, as they stood up in total disbelief.

"Well, I'll be damned! That can't be our sister?" Jeremiah said.

"Yep, that's her, the mighty Siren herself," Alexander answered.

Their reactions made Lori blush. She smiled, when she noticed Lucas. He stood up and gazed lovingly at his stunning lady.

"Wow…no way. Is that a smile? Is Lo actually smiling? Bruh, we have to keep you around for a few millennia. We must get this on camera," Jeremiah suggested.

"Shut up Jeremiah. Lucas, pay no attention to these fools. They're always trying to provoke me in some way or another," Lori said playfully. Abigail rounded up the rest of the family to witness Lori's fabulous makeover. Everyone marveled, which made her a little uneasy.

"You look amazing, sweetie. Make sure you work that Black Girl Magic tonight and let Luc work some of his magic on you, too," Nora said jokingly.

Nezera stood expressionless and not the least bit impressed. The rest of the family was simply amazed to see Lori all dolled up. She hadn't looked this sophisticated in years. Abigail snapped a few pictures of Lori and Lucas to capture the moment.

"Dinner is ready guys," Nora announced.

"Dinner, I thought we were going out," Lucas answered.

"We will, trust me. For now, I prepared an amazing meal for us. We can enjoy great conversation and some of the best wine," Lori suggested.

"Well, I have no problem with that," Lucas replied.

Lori took him by the hand and led him to the plateau where a delicious meal awaited. Twinkling lights were strung everywhere, and the table marveled with candlelight. Lucas was in awe of the beautiful surroundings and the effort they put into preparing such a romantic evening.

"You did all of this for me?" Lucas asked.

"Well, I wanted to surprise you," she said.

"Thank you so much. No one has ever done anything like this for me," Lucas claimed.

"There's a first time for everything," Lori replied, kissing him sweetly on the lips.

"I am a bit surprised, though. I thought you would have to beat the girls away with a stick," Lori joked.

"Not as often as you might think," Lucas replied with a grin.

"Well, I'm pleased to have you all to myself. I would hate to have to snatch up one of those thirsty females and show off my dark side," she kidded.

"Now, now…we can't have that," Lucas replied.

He politely pulled out Lori's chair. Joshua, Nora, Jeremiah, Abigail, and Alexander were all staring through the glass, observing with anticipation. Lori glanced over and waved them off, so they could enjoy their lovely evening…alone.

"We can take it from here guys, thank you very much," she stated.

As Lucas began eating, he said to Lori, "Are you planning to eat something or are you going to sit there, staring at me?"

"Perhaps I am looking to serve you up as my main course later tonight," she answered flirtatiously. "But seriously though, blood drooling from the corners of my mouth would ruin your appetite."

"Oh, no it wouldn't. I'm interested in learning about every part of you, baby. Not just your human side, your predatory side as well…all of you," Lucas said.

"Wow, so you're saying nothing about my family frightens you?" Lori asked.

"Are you saying I should be frightened? Maybe, I don't see you all as vicious, bloodsucking demons," Lucas stated.

"I don't know, perhaps you should be frightened. Understand Luc, aspects of vampirism exists within us. It makes us dangerous and unpredictable. We're constantly at odds with our very nature and it's extremely taxing. In many ways, we are more of a threat to humanity because we exist beyond the shadows of darkness.

"But you're not cold-blooded and you all have taken an oath to defend mankind," Lucas remarked.

"Sometimes the oath is not enough when the thirst takes hold. It takes hold and completely robs us of our sense of reason. Trust me, I know what I'm talking about," Lori explained.

"You sound like you've had those experiences," Lucas replied.

"I've been there a time or two. We all have experienced the thirst and it's not something we take lightly. When the blood-rage comes over us, our predatory instincts are what drives us. We have no concept of morality or compassion," Lori explained.

"Well, you all seem to have plenty of self-control," Lucas stated.

"It comes from years of practice and lots of self-discipline," Lori replied.

"So, are most of your kind, Hunters?" Lucas inquired.

"There are those of us who are Hunters and those of us who just want to live in peace and harmony, bound by the oath. Over the years, we've managed to replenish our numbers by developing our own sophisticated society. Our technological advancements are second to none. I'm what you call a "Saber Siren." Sirens are the all-female, fight force of the Blood Sabers. To become a Siren or a Saber you have to undergo various rituals. For us, it's not as simple as receiving a bite to the neck. We are a tight community and extremely exclusive," Lori explained.

"You still haven't told me how or why you fit into this story, Lorelei," Lucas stated.

Her eyes began to flutter with astonishment as Lucas said her full name. "I haven't been called that name in a long while." At first, she hesitated, unsure of how much of the truth she was willing to divulge.

"There was a time when I was nothing more than a house slave, living on a plantation. Then the worst thing that could ever happen to a slave, happened to me. I fell deeply in love. We were not allowed to fall in love or have intimate feelings. We were nothing more than flesh for sale. Nez and I were sold into servitude at birth. One day I met a man, this beautiful, beautiful man. We dreamed of a life beyond the bowels of enslavement and torture. One night, after months of contemplation, we decided to make our escape under the covers of nightfall. We were tracked and hunted down like dogs by bounty hunters…vampires. The man I loved with all my heart, was taken from me. Nez and I were beaten and raped within inches of our lives. The bastards wouldn't feed on us for fear of turning us. They said, "A nigger could never fathom the meaning of immortality or the concept of living forever. Let these nigga-bitches perish." We were seconds away from death, when Joshua appeared from the shadows offering us a second chance, another life. That night, he turned us and accepted us as his own. He gave me the powers to avenge the love I was denied and since then, I've known only one thing, and that's the life of a Siren. A huntress of the night who knows no fear, no emotion,

no compassion and no remorse when I kill. I'm a lethal instrument of rage and skill," Lori explained.

"So, what are you telling me, I'm dining with a black Kate Beckinsale?" Lucas asked.

"Luc, I'm serious. Our lives nor our existence are for the faint of heart. Like vampires, we are predators beyond time. I have hunted and I have killed humans and vampires alike. I'm not proud of it, but I'm not ashamed either," Lori said.

"Wow, this is kind of deep for a first date, don't you think?" Lucas asked with sarcasm.

"Is it too much for you?" She asked.

"No, I'm glad you shared your story. However, I don't think Nez is as excepting of me as the rest of your family," Lucas claimed.

"No worries, she's just highly protective of me, like any other annoying big sister. I haven't had a man in many years," Lori expressed.

Although, Lucas was not entirely convinced by Lori's explanation of her sister's attitude, he smiled and said, "Okay baby."

"Well, enough with the heavy. How was your meal?" She asked with a smile.

"It was absolutely divine. My compliments to the chef," Lucas said.

"I am certainly glad everything turned out okay," Lori said with relief.

"I guess you've had a few centuries to perfect your many skills, because you're a real beast in the kitchen. Downtown should be jumping off tonight. Let's hang out a bit," Lucas insisted.

"I don't know if we should. We suspect Ross's goons has you under surveillance, but what the hell...let's live a little. Plus, I've been waiting to experience more of your smooth, dance moves," Lori teased.

They left the house and made their way downtown. Lucas was correct when he said downtown was jumping. For a while, there was back-to-back traffic. Plenty of people were out and about, enjoying the nightlife. The two of them ended up at a club called "The Red Room", which was appropriate, since Lori was wearing a sexy, red and black, laced dress. The club was packed. They found themselves in the middle of the floor, dancing closely. Song after song, they were totally oblivious to everyone else. In their minds, everything was moving in slow motion.

As the night progressed, they made their way to the rooftop for some intimate, quality time...totally unaware they were under surveillance.

Looking into Lucas's eyes, Lori said, "Thank you so much."

Unsure as to why, Lucas asked, "For what, babe?"

"It's been a while since I've been on a real date. Quite frankly, I don't do this often and I haven't had these feelings in a very long time," she admitted.

"It's no wonder I haven't found the right women, she's been on lockdown for the last two hundred years," Lucas teased.

During a brief moment of silence, they gazed at each other. They were completely drawn into one another. As they were about to share another kiss, they became distracted by the noise around them. They giggled as their foreheads gently touched.

"I would love a drink," Lori said.

"What do you have in mind?" Lucas asked.

"Hmmm, a chocolate martini sounds good," Lori suggested.

"Coming right up," Lucas replied.

He hurried to the bar on the ground floor. Lucas had a smooth way of maneuvering through a crowd. Finally, he ordered a chocolate martini, along with his usual drink. He threw back the shot of Washington Apple, grabbed his Royal Flush and martini, then proceeded towards the roof. Before he could reach the door, he was abruptly interrupted by a couple of men dressed in suits. His drinks spilled as he was shoved and thrown into the alley.

"Who are you guys and what the fuck do you want? Oh and you owe me for those drinks," Lucas demanded.

As they began to surround him, one of them replied, "Let's just say, you have sparked the interest of my employer. He wants you hand-delivered, wrapped in a little bow. In what particular state we make our delivery, is totally up to you," the man said sternly.

"You know, I thought vampires were bold enough and fully capable of doing their own dirty work. I didn't think they needed their so-called flunkies to do it for them," Lucas answered.

The man approached Lucas, visibly infuriated by his comment. He delivered a violent blow to Lucas's abdomen, dropping him to his knees.

"Perhaps you have the wrong idea. Clearly, there are five of us and only one of you, so I would check the insults and sarcasm," the man demanded.

Regaining his breath, Lucas said, "Is that it? I think I might enjoy those odds."

The man laughed boldly. He was ready to strike again, but Lucas quickly responded by brutally striking the man's groin and inner thigh. He then connected with a vicious, rising head-butt to his chin and face. Blood was gushing from the man's mouth as he fell violently to the pavement. Underestimating Lucas's capabilities, the other four men looked in awe, as their head comrade hit the concrete. They immediately turned their gaze upon Lucas, but it was already too late. He didn't wait for them to respond. Lucas quickly began fighting each of them, utilizing his hand-to-hand combat skills. Locking, throwing, striking, kicking, and stomping. Lucas made each of them pay for attacking him and attempting to capture him.

Lucas grabbed one of the men by the throat and said, "When you see your boss, tell him I said, if he wants me, he needs to grow a sack and come get me." After releasing the man, he suddenly received a mighty blow to the back of his head and fell face-first onto the pavement.

"Dually noted," Drea responded, towering over Lucas.

She tried to grab him, but sensed the presence of someone approaching. Unexpectedly, Lori emerged from the darkness, laying hands on Drea. She slammed her against the brick wall, as Drea manifested her hideous, vampire features. The two struggled back and forth with neither gaining the upper hand. They were at a stalemate.

"My, my, my…it's been a long time, Huntress. How have you been?" Drea sneered.

Lori answered, "Actually, I was just starting to enjoy myself when you and your peckerwood proxies showed up."

"Well...we aim to please, bitch!" Drea yelled.

She advanced and took a swipe at Lori with her sharp claws. Lori grabbed her by the wrist, countering the attacks and delivered numerous brutal strikes. Drea was lying motionless, flat on her face. Out of nowhere, Alexander and Abigail appeared in a black Mercedes SUV.

"Get in!" Alexander shouted.

Lori quickly grabbed Lucas and lifted him to his feet and they fled the scene.

"What are you guys doing here?" Lori asked.

"Come on sis, you know daddy wouldn't let you two out of his sight without chaperones to cover your asses," Alexander answered.

"How did they find you?" Abigail asked.

"Well, they obviously have eyes on us. I would assume they have access to traffic cams, city grids...the whole nine," Lori stated.

"Wait. How is that possible?" Lucas asked.

"It's what we told you, they have their claws into just about everything…finance, innovative technologies, politics and even real estate. Their influence extends throughout the entire planet," Alex explained.

The Slades were extremely careful as they pulled into their storage facility. They switched cars to cover their tracks, just in case they were being followed. As they pulled up, Joshua along with Nora, Jeremiah, and Nezera were waiting impatiently.

"Are you two alright?" Joshua asked.

"Yeah, we're fine. Look, Ross has assets and cattle-brand units in the area. We weren't followed, but it will only be a matter of time before he finds us," Lori explained.

"I guess it's time I entered the game. The two of you should stay put for now," Joshua insisted.

"Lo, that means you, too. Now, Ross knows you will never leave Lucas, so you'll have to stay out of Drea's pathway," Nora ordered.

"Okay fine, but we still need to find Ross's location," Lori suggested.

"Leave that to us, Lo. We'll find him," Jeremiah said. They headed out the door and into the midst of the night, as Lori led Lucas upstairs.

Lucas's wound to the back of his head was not yet healing. Lori applied a cold towel to his injury.

"My head hurts like hell," Lucas groaned.

She cleaned the wound and relieved the swelling. Lucas immediately began to heal.

"Who the hell was that bitch who slugged me?" Lucas asked.

"Her name is Drea. She's Ross's second-in-command. We've had run-ins with her before. A real doll, isn't she?" Lori said.

"How did you know I was in trouble?" Lucas inquired.

"I tracked your scent and used my hearing to scope the surrounding area," Lori explained.

"Well, I'm certainly grateful you showed up when you did," Lucas said.

"You don't ever have to worry, babe. I've got your back," Lori replied.

"What did I do to deserve such a loyal and beautiful woman?" Lucas questioned.

"Well…one, I'm no ordinary woman and two, I know your heart. It's worth protecting," Lori stated.

"Well, it's still refreshing to know I have such a fierce woman by my side," Lucas stated. She gave him a kiss on the forehead and said, "Try and get some sleep, love. You're under the protection of the Silver Fang. They would have to come through all of us to get to you. Believe that."

8

The Re-occurrence

Lori changed into a dark tank top and shorts and headed toward the computer room. The Slade's Informational Center was extremely advanced. They used state-of-the-art holographic technology, which was far more cutting-edge than technology used by the military. They could access classified information needed to find their targets by using an array of informational servers. Abigail, Jeremiah and Nora were busy searching for news of strange occurrences surrounding Ross's arrival.

Lori entered the room and asked, "Do you have anything yet?"

"Not yet, but there have been numerous mysterious occurrences from the last eight weeks. A man and a woman were brutally slain in the park five miles from downtown. The autopsy report stated their blood was completely drained from their bodies. The authorities deemed it a vicious, animal attack. They're searching for large animals in the area," Abigail explained.

"Those cops are full of shit. It's not even a good cover story. Wasn't that around the time Ross made his appearance?" Lori asked.

"Yes, it's spot on," Abigail answered.

"Check for any abandoned warehouses and storage facilities with underground access. Those bastards will need somewhere to lay low. There can only be a few of these facilities with that capability," Lori suggested.

Meanwhile, as Lori and the rest of her family continued to conduct their investigation into Ross's whereabouts, Lucas rested his eyes. While sleeping, flashbacks of war and violence, along with images of his parents' death plagued his mind, but this dream was a lot more descriptive. Clearly, Lucas was regaining some of his memory. Scared out of his mind, he jumped out of bed. He ran outside to the training plateau, where he set up three projectile pillars. He trained vigorously to overcome his frustrations. He tied the blindfold over his eyes to enhance his other senses. With amazing form and precision, Lucas threw each metal star at the pillars hitting the targets accurately.

"Very impressive, Lucas. You've come a long way in eight weeks. As you know, killing a vampire is quite the feat for a human. But then again, you're not the average human are you?" Nezera expressed.

She stood at the door as Lucas removed his blindfold. "Why are you here? Tension has plagued us since I set foot in this house. Perhaps you can explain your obvious dislike for me," Lucas suggested.

"Maybe, I'm not convinced you're up to the task," Nezera answered.

"Are you referring to killing vampires or my commitment to Lori?" Lucas asked. "Both. My sister and the rest of my family believes in you. So blindly, they're willing to risk everything to protect you. The truth is, we've been here before...you, Lori and I," Nezera claimed.

"What exactly are you talking about?" Lucas asked.

"So, she didn't tell you?" Nez stated.

"Tell me what?" Lucas asked.

"Come with me," she said, as she led him to the basement. She pulled the cloth from the frame, revealing the portrait Lori held dear to her heart. Lucas stood gazing in shock and disbelief.

"What is this, some kind of joke?" Lucas asked.

"No, not at all. She drew this painting sixty years ago in remembrance of her past love who was captured," Nezera claimed.

The painting was of an African American man, dressed in seventeenth century clothing. The mysterious man looked exactly like Lucas.

"Lucas, this life is not your first life. You existed three centuries ago, as a Re-occurrence or Echo. Let me guess, you feel an unspoken connection to Lori. A feeling of familiarity that cannot be understood or explained," Nez stated.

"How do you know this?" Lucas asked.

"The year was 1787. You were a slave brought to work on the plantation down in New Orleans. Of course, we were fully human back then. My sister was captivated by you the moment she laid eyes upon you.

You convinced both of us to escape to freedom with you, risking everything," Nez explained. Lucas stood listening to Nezera's words with great sadness. He could no longer deny what he realized had to be the truth.

"Did she tell you we were caught, raped and beaten within an inch of our lives?" Nezera asked.

"Yes, but she told me that the man she loved was also killed in the process," Lucas added.

"No, you were dragged away, leaving us to die. After we were turned that night, Lo spent the next two and a half years searching for you. When she finally found you, you were happily married with two beautiful children living the freedom you so often talked about. She couldn't bring herself to intrude, as she watched her whole world crumble before her eyes. As much as she loved you, she wanted the best for you. I had to witness my baby sister die inside for two hundred years over the loss of you," she stated.

As Nezera continued, her eyes began to water and tears streamed down her face. Lucas lowered his head in sadness, as he listened to every word.

"Many years later, Lo consulted a witch seer. She prophesized the man fate had once stolen from her, would return in another life. He would bear the same striking resemblance to his ancestor. It's like déjà vu and yet again, we're sacrificing everything for you. Even now, you still pose a threat to those I hold dear," Nezera exclaimed.

"So, it's up to you to decide who and what she deserves? You don't even know me, yet you're making assumptions based on what transpired in a past life. Lori swore all of you to secrecy, didn't she?" Lucas asked.

Nezera gazed at Lucas, and then looked away knowing he was right. Lori had asked everyone in the house to not divulge the painting or the circumstances that surrounded it. She made all of them swear to never tell.

"Lucas, you don't belong here. The only shame is admitting it before it's too late," Nezera claimed.

"I understand you want to protect your sister and your family, but are you sure you're going about it the right way? I have no intentions of hurting your sister or any of you. All of you have opened my eyes and rescued me in the process. I am extremely grateful for that. But if you believe I pose a serious threat to your family, I'll leave," Lucas stated.

Lori overheard the conversion from upstairs. "Damn you, Nez...damn you," she uttered under her breath.

The others stared at her, as Lori abruptly ran from the room and down to the basement. She appeared on the stairway, looking down at them.

"What the hell do you think you're doing, Nez?" Lori asked angrily.

Lucas and Nezera were surprised to see Lori.

"He deserved to know the truth," Nezera claimed. Lucas ran up the staircase passing Lori without saying a word. She grabbed his arm and he gently pulled away. "You should have told me," Lucas replied.

"I know, I just...I just needed some time to gather my thoughts. I couldn't find the right words and was afraid you wouldn't understand. I'm not even sure I truly understand. Lucas please, please don't leave," Lori begged.

"I have to," Lucas said as he hurried upstairs to pack his things. Lori confronted Nezera, disgusted by the very sight of her.

"Why, Nez? And don't tell me it's because he deserved to know the truth. This is about you and what you believe my life should be. Who are you to dictate who I should love?" Lori yelled.

"Lo, it's about all of us. Your love for this mortal is going to get us all killed, just like before. You just can't see it or maybe you choose not to," Nezera declared.

"You know what I see, Nez...I see happiness when it's all said and done. This is my second chance at a beautiful life with Lucas and if you ruin my chances with him, I will never forgive your betrayal. You hear me...I will never, ever forgive you!" Lori yelled.

She hurried upstairs with hopes of preventing Lucas from leaving. She burst into the room, as he continued packing. He heard her footsteps as she drew nearer. "So, you knew? You had me under surveillance all this time. You've known who I was all along...this so-called Echo...you all knew. Who was I back then, babe? What was my name?" Lucas asked.

126

"Louis. Louis Stevens," she answered softly. "He was...I mean, you were a great man. Very loving, understanding, wise and strong. The same as you are now. It ripped my heart from my chest when I lost him...when I lost you. It was impossible to fully give my heart to another because I could not see past you. It was my burden to bear," Lori explained tearfully.

"I don't know if I'm the same man you lost all those years ago," Lucas said, slowly turning toward.

She gently held his face and looked deep into his eyes. "You are, babe. You can't see it, but I can. I truly can," Lori proclaimed.

"I...I don't know. I just need some time and distance. I need time to figure things out and I can't do it here," Lucas said.

"Lucas, please don't leave. You have no idea how long I've waited for you. I cannot...I can't just let you walk away. I don't want to lose you again. I can only protect you here," Lori replied.

"Lo, I just need one day. I need twenty-four hours to get my head right," Lucas pleaded.

Lori stood at the front door, along with Nora, Abigail and Alexander as Lucas prepared to leave. Nora attempted to convince Lucas to stay, but his mind was made up.

"That girl up there loves you. She's waited for you for the last two hundred years and I know you love her, as well. It's written all over your face. In her defense, Lori was terrified to tell you, in fear of seeing this very look on your face. Luc please, we can't protect you out there," Nora stated.

Lucas understood the risk he was taking. His stubborn nature wouldn't allow him to budge on his decision. He expressed his sincerest gratitude to each of them for their hospitality and support. They looked on, in sadness, as he got in the taxi and disappeared out of sight. Nezera was staring down from her bedroom window as the car pulled away. Suddenly, she could feel Lori's presence. She was standing at Nezera's door with sheer disdain in her eyes. Tears streaming down her face and anger burning in her blood.

"You know what they say, sis...if you love something, let it go," Nezera said arrogantly.

Lori, not breaking stride, snatched her sister by the back of the neck. In one swift motion, she slung her violently against the wall, like a ragdoll. Nezera was managing to hold her own, but Lori's offensive attacks, encompassed with her rage, made it nearly impossible for Nezera to bear.

Lori held her sister by the throat and screamed, "You had no right! I trusted you and you betrayed me!"

"You gonna to kill me too, Siren?" Nezera gasped, struggling to speak.

Nora, Abigail and Alexander rushed upstairs, as the commotion between Lori and Nezera shook the house. They desperately tried to contain the situation.

Nora ran in the room and pulled Lori off of Nezera. She stood between them and demanded, "Stop! That is quite enough! We have no time for this sibling rivalry shit. Nez, you had no right. You were sworn to secrecy, the same as the rest of us. Telling him the truth only caused more confusion. You don't realize what you might have cost us and your sister. I suggest, if you want to remain a part of this household, you'd better help us find this boy!" Nora shouted.

"You have compromised my relationship with Lucas, not to mention, his safety. If something happens to him, you will have betrayed me for the very last time," Lori said angrily.

Nezera's face was covered with tears and her mouth was full of blood. She came to terms with her mistake and the havoc she wreaked on her family. As they left the room, Nezera stood in silence. Her shame denied her the right to speak. Quickly, Lori and Nora rushed down to the basement. Lori began loading weapons into a very large duffle bag.

"What are you preparing to do, Lo?" Nora asked.

"Whatever I can. Three weeks ago, I implanted a small GPS tracker node in Lucas's left arm as he slept," Lori explained.

"Wow...damn girl. I don't know what to say. That's some stalker shit. You implanted your man with a tracking device?" Nora stated.

"We don't have time for a lesson in morals right now. He's been gone for almost an hour and I pray he made it to his apartment. I'll start there. You guys stay here, I'll track him down," Lori demanded.

"No. You and I will do this together," Nora said.

"I don't need a chaperone, Nora. I can do this solo," Lori insisted.

"Not today. Two Sirens on the trail will cover more ground than one. You'll need my help. Plus, Ross and his goons are on patrol. Lastly, I am the matriarch of this household and second-in-command. This is the order of your commanding officer," Nora demanded.

Lori had no choice in the matter. Nora was tagging along whether she agreed or not.

As they loaded the weapons in the SUV, Nora phoned Joshua. He answered, "Do you guys have a location?"

"Abigail and Alexander are tapped into the city grids and are still searching. However, right now, we have another problem. Lucas left in a cab about an hour ago. Nez revealed the painting to him and the whole truth about his identity. He's hurt, confused and all alone. We couldn't convince him to stay. Lori and I are on our way to his apartment and we'll continue tracking from there," Nora explained.

"Alright, do what you can. Just be very careful, because downtown is already becoming crowded. Remember, the City Festival is today. As the sun sets, there's no doubt Ross and his bloodsuckers will be on the hunt for Luc. We can't partake in a public firefight among crowds of innocent people," Joshua declared.

"I understand, babe," Nora answered.

"Please, please be careful and I love you," Joshua professed.

"I love you, too," Nora responded as she hopped in the front passenger seat.

Lori sped out of the driveway. They headed toward Lucas's apartment. It was a race against time to find him. The question remained, who would locate him first? As Lori drove, she felt solely responsible for the situation at hand.

"I should not have kept the truth from him. I drove him away. The only man I have ever loved reappears and I can't be honest with him," Lori said.

"No, Lori. You wanted to protect him, just like you're doing right now. Lucas is young, but incredibly wise. He will come around. Just give him time to settle his mind a bit. He's been thrown into a world of horrors he never knew existed and is learning more about himself in the process. He's your soulmate and you are his. I know the signs. Lo, he will be yours again," Nora reassured.

"Thanks Nora...you always keep me focused," Lori said.

"Well, that's what matriarchs are for, my dear. Trust me, everything will be just fine," Nora insisted.

As they continued to search the city, Joshua informed Jeremiah of the escalated situation.

"It seems as if your wife couldn't keep her fury against Lucas contained. She showed him the painting and revealed everything. Now, Lucas is missing," Joshua explained.

"Damn. I wish I could say I'm surprised, but we all knew from the day his return was prophesized, Nez wasn't looking forward to it. I've had so many conversations with her about her sister's life and she still doesn't get it. Nez is so headstrong and stuck in her ways," Jeremiah reasoned.

"So right now, we have Alexander and Abigail locating Ross's whereabouts from home. They will call us when they've spotted him. Lori and Nora are tracking Lucas," Joshua stated.

9

Festival of Horrors

The sun was setting, as nightfall approached. When suddenly, Joshua and Jeremiah caught wind of a vampire. Jeremiah quickly pulled the SUV on the side of the road and began to track the scent on foot. It emanated from a nearby park downtown, where crowds of people congregated. Ross was awaiting Joshua's presence. Jeremiah kept his distance, as the standoff ensued.

"The great Joshua Slade...Silver Fang. It's good to finally meet you. I've heard so much about you and your family. I must say, your reputation precedes you," Ross declared sarcastically.

"Well, I don't know how good it is. I usually have the urge to slaughter your kind, first chance I get," Joshua answered.

"So, let's keep this very simple. You know why I'm here and what I want. Why don't you just hand over the Captain? There's no need for our first-time meeting to be unpleasant," Ross insisted.

"Why should I turn him over to you? So you can vivisect him, then harvest him for your pitiful, ruthless scheme to make you and your kind indestructible? You were in such a hurry to knock off Roman Shaw, you could never figure out where Night-worth was stored, could you?" Joshua asked.

"I knew where it was," Ross answered arrogantly.

"Oh, so you realized the only way Shaw could fully test the serum was by injecting himself, using his own body as a science experiment. While you were busy murdering him, you were destroying the very thing you came for," Joshua proclaimed. Ross couldn't deny that fact. His plan wasn't as ingenious as he had hoped.

"Well bright boy, you seem to know quite a bit of information. You're much smarter than I thought. Let me ask you this...do you actually think humans will accept a hybrid, off-spring strain such as yourself? Your lust for blood matches ours. You're lurking in the night just as we do. Yet, you think because you choose to ignore the hunger in your blood, you're righteous among the living. Look at them, nothing more than cattle waiting to be devoured, as their world grows dimmer by the second. Soon, the shadows will become the new norm and the para-enhanced will lay claim to their existence. We are the evolved and ultimately, this entire planet will be ours. Right now, I am offering you the opportunity to save you and your clans. Look the other way and give me the boy. Either you join us or join them, as they are annihilated," Ross declared.

"Join you, huh? You must think I am a fool. You see, I'm old school. Me and mine have a lingering respect for the living. I've witnessed your kind slaughter the innocent for centuries…just for sport. Believing you are morally superior in the eyes of evolution but, you're not. You exist as rodents squabbling about in the shadows with no remorse and not a shred of respect for the lives you take. Save the speech because I'm not buying it. I've put down many like you, wanting to rise above their stations. You're a turned, full-blood wannabe. I was born a Saber and I'll die one. So, if you want to live another day, I would advise you to cancel the contract on the boy…leave town, and stick to what you know," Joshua demanded.

"You have no idea who you're dealing with, Slade. Your fine words are talking you out of peace and into your own extinction. Rest assured, you will learn to respect me, boy. Once I slaughter your precious human, I will turn all of my attention to you and your family of half-breeds," Ross promised. Joshua reached for his gun, loaded with silver ammunition. Ross quickly noticed and said, "Careful, we wouldn't want to endanger the lives of these innocent civilians, now would we?"

"I thought they were insignificant to you?" Joshua reiterated.

"So be it!" Ross shouted, as he drew his handgun and shot an innocent bystander walking by, which resulted in chaos and panic throughout the crowd. Everyone began running, as the man's body hit the ground. The blood from his wound splattered, covering the grass. Screams flooded the area, as the innocent fled for their lives.

Before Joshua and Jeremiah could draw their weapons, Ross grabbed a woman, using her as a human shield. "Do you want to watch another one die?" Ross asked.

Joshua drew his weapon and tried to aim, but, there were too many bystanders in his line of fire. Ross threw his hostage to the ground and took off running. His speed allowed him to evade Joshua's gunfire. Suddenly, the sound of police sirens dominated the screams resonating from the commotion. "Josh, let's go!" Jeremiah yelled. Using their super speed, they fled the scene. As they approached their vehicle, Joshua was very agitated. "We need to track Lori and Nora. If Lucas falls into the hands of that maniac, we can kiss this fight for humanity goodbye." He declared.

Meanwhile, Lori and Nora arrived at Lucas's apartment and he was nowhere to be found. Joshua was frantically calling Nora.

"Is he there?" Joshua asked breathing heavily.

"No, he's not...he's not here," she repeated.

They searched Lucas's place for clues to his whereabouts. His lingering scent was the only lead they could depend on.

"It seems we have to do this the hard way. Most likely, he's in the midst of the City Festival," Lori stated.

"In order to find him, we must coordinate. Stay on your communicators and earpieces. Meet me and Jeremiah downtown," Joshua ordered.

"Will do," Nora answered.

In the meantime, Lucas was walking alone in the midst of the crowded City Festival. He was oblivious that Ross and his team of bloodsuckers were among the festival's inhabitants. The sun had set and Lucas was focused on the events that led him to this very moment. He couldn't help but feel his entire existence was one huge lie. Lucas watched as happy families and lovers enjoyed the festivities. All of a sudden, sadness commenced and he began to resent the simplicity of their lives. No complications and no lies...only love and happiness surrounded him. As fireworks sounded off, Lucas reacted in sheer terror. This was the exact feeling he remembered as a child. His body flinched as they exploded in the sky. His flashbacks were as vivid as his dreams. The visions were so realistic, Lucas couldn't distinguish between the two. He grabbed his head, moaning from the throbbing pain he felt behind his eyes. He could see the dreadful images violently massacre his parents. Clearly, it was Ross's face that appeared in the darkness. He and his band of vampires decapitated

Lucas's father, then raped and shot his mother. As the panic attack continued, Lucas reached in his pocket for his anxiety medication, but the bottle was empty. He could hear his parents screaming, which made his headache even more unbearable. Lucas's eyes watered and tears began to flow uncontrollably.

No one noticed as he dropped to his knees, weakened by pain and sorrow. With blurred vision, he lifted his head and saw two dark shadows rushing toward him.

"No more! Please, no more!" He cried loudly.

"Luc, it's alright...you're going to be alright," Lori reassured.

"Lucas, you're having a panic attack," Nora explained, as she rolled up his right sleeve and injected an anti-anxiety sedative into his arm.

"You're my dark angel, Lo...always coming to my rescue. How did you two find me?" Lucas whispered.

"It's complicated," Lori admitted.

Immediately, Lori and Nora sensed the presence of vampires lurking in the midst.

"We must go. Can you walk, babe?" Lori asked. Regaining his strength, Lucas rose to his feet with Lori's help and replied, "Yeah, I can make it."

As they prepared to leave, they were instantly surrounded by a squad of vampires.

"We need a quick diversion," Nora whispered to Lori.

Lori pulled out her nine millimeter handgun and fired two shots at the ground. Suddenly, the crowd panicked and scattered with fear. The vampires found it extremely difficult to navigate and locate their target. Nora and Lori didn't waste any time getting out of there with Lucas in tow.

"I saw it, I saw it...the whole thing. I remember everything so clearly. I saw Ross and his goons murder my parents," Lucas murmured as they fled.

"Come on Lucas, we must keep moving," Lori insisted.

As the vampires chased them through the frightened crowd, they began to throw and attack anyone who crossed their path. One of the henchmen grabbed an innocent man by the throat and chucked him into a festival display. Soon thereafter, each vampire began unloading fire…wounding and killing civilians. Nora, Lori, and Lucas continued navigating through the horrific pandemonium. Nora and Lori returned fire as they protected and shielded Lucas. They managed to take out some of the vampires who tried to converge on their position. While holding off the horde of bloodsuckers, Nora informed Joshua of their position.

"We are pinned down and innocent bystanders are being killed," Nora confirmed.

"We are almost at your location," Joshua stated.

The situation became more turbulent. Police sirens sounded as they arrived on the scene and were no match for Ross's henchmen. As they fired their weapons, the bullets did not faze the vampires. They began firing back at the policemen and their vehicles, murdering the officers without breaking a sweat. The constant firing detonated each of the police cars. The vampires were virtually indestructible.

"My God!" Lucas shouted.

The situation quickly escalated into a massacre.

Lori handed Lucas a sidearm weapon and said, "It's loaded with silver nitrate and a round is already chambered. Be prepared to run as quickly as you can. We can't wait around for Joshua and Jeremiah."

"What? I'm not leaving you here!" Lucas yelled.

"It's alright, we got this," Nora said crouching to avoid stray bullets.

"Go, I'll find you," Lori insisted, leaning in to kiss Lucas. "You damn well better," he replied.

Lucas took off running through the chaos. Nora and Lori continued covering him until he was out of sight. He fled the scene with a crowd of terrified bystanders. Lucas managed to assist some of the helpless victims, but he didn't make it far. A bloodsucker was trailing close behind him and Lucas ran as fast as he could. He noticed the city burning around him and felt responsible for the victims who perished. Suddenly, Lucas was being choked. He was reaching his sidearm but was thrown into some garbage cans. He stood up and noticed his enemy running towards him, so he braced himself and stood grounded in his position.

The vampire charged and tackled Lucas into the window of a local Army-Navy Surplus store. The glass shattered, as they continued to struggle. Lucas was bleeding profusely from his head. The vampire continued to beat and punch him into oblivion. He continued to resist the vampire's strength, while being tossed around. Lucas snatched a cleaver knife from the wall and began swinging at his enemy. Using any means necessary to destroy the monster. The vampire blocked the blade, and then delivered a shocking, backhand swing to Lucas's face. Lucas staggered from the devastating blow, while spitting out blood. He gathered his strength to wield a bat towards his enemy. He was unsuccessful, as the vampire's strength and speed greatly overpowered him. All of a sudden, the vampire pinned Lucas against the wall and attempted to sidekick him. As Lucas evaded contact, his enemy violently kicked through the wall. Lucas delivered a hard-swinging haymaker to the bloodsucker's head, followed by a springing jump kick. He landed perfectly, as the vampire fell hard on the floor.

Suddenly, everything slowed as Lucas gained clarity and calmness within. A revelation took hold of his mind. He instantly knew what he had to do and how he needed to do it. He could hear Joshua's words of martial wisdom echoing throughout his mind. The vampire rose to his feet and launched a brick directly at Lucas, who smashed it into fragments with his fist. He was now becoming more aware of his fierce power and abilities. His confidence increased, as he demonstrated courage and impermeable posture. Agitated by his newfound valor, the vampire tossed a metal chair, but Lucas stretched backwards, kicked into the air, and catapulted the chair behind him. The bloodsucker grabbed Lucas's knife from the floor and charged at him, swinging the blade, but Lucas quickly evaded the weapon. Moving continuously, he managed to strike, hit and maneuver, while avoiding the vampire's deadly path.

Lucas grabbed a cleaver knife from the floor and attempted to disarm the vampire. It was now an even struggle…both fighting to the death. They were slashing, cutting and hacking, when Lucas finally gained the upper hand. He continued to induce the destruction of his enemy. He severed the vampire's hand and it disintegrated into combustible ash. Lucas proceeded to strategically slash every major artery in the bloodsucker's body. The smell of blood and ash lingered in the air, as the vampire groaned in agony. Lucas gazed down into the bloodsucker's eyes, while recalling the horrifying events of the night his parents were slaughtered. The monster that lay before him had severed his father's head. The flashback quickly magnified Lucas's anger.

"I remember you," Lucas declared, while brutally slashing his enemy's throat. The vampire's blood splattered on the floor and his body fell limp and lifeless. All of a sudden, the body combusted and disintegrated into ash. Feeling relieved and content, Lucas stared at the blood-covered weapon.

The chaos had ceased and an eerie silence fell upon him. As Lucas made his way through the rubble, he felt a stinging pinch in his neck. He reached up and removed a sleep dart, but it was too late. He was already feeling the effects, as his knees buckled and his body caved. Through blurred vision, he noticed pale-skinned figures approaching him in dark clothing. Lucas had finally laid eyes on Dorian Ross for the first time. Drea and other members of his crew stood quickly, peering down at him.

"Mr. Shaw. It's nice to meet your acquaintance, yet again," Ross sneered.

"You bastard," Lucas mumbled.

"Yes. That's me," Ross answered smugly.

Lucas's eyelids became very heavy and soon faded to black. Ross quickly ordered his goons to remove Lucas's body. He knew the Slades would be on his trail and without hesitation, they were.

10

A Captured Soldier

The Slades approached the aftermath. Lori and Nora were accompanied by Joshua and Jeremiah, who arrived in the nick of time. While observing the ruins of the store, they each gathered clues using extra-sensory perception.

"Lucas put down one of Ross's goons before he was captured. Damn, that boy got steel," Jeremiah stated in awe.

"This is where they captured him," Joshua claimed, as he bent down taking a closer look.

"Can you smell that?" Joshua asked.

"Yeah, it smells like chloral hydrate," Nora answered.

"Yep. They shot Lucas with it and took him soon afterwards," Joshua explained.

Meanwhile, Lori stood motionless in the demolished store. Engrossed with anger, she clenched her fists. Her eyes gleamed with a blazing flare that could cut steel. Her fangs were clearly elongated, and she was undoubtedly heated. The love of her life had been stolen from her, once again. Suddenly, they heard police sirens from a block away.

"It's time to roll out!" Joshua shouted.

Nora quickly grabbed Lori, shaking her from the enraged trance. They swiftly joined the guys and fled the scene.

They returned home to find Alexander, Abigail, and Nezera eagerly waiting for updates.

Dashing into the house, Joshua yelled, "Do you have anything on them yet?"

"We've crossed-referenced a couple of addresses for abandoned storage facilities with subterranean access. So far, there are five of these facilities in the area. We would never locate them in time," Abigail feared.

"We won't have to. While Lucas was sleeping, I implanted a small tracking nod under his flesh. We should have no trouble tracking him," Lori stated.

She handed Abigail the tracking receiver. It would boost the signal in order to locate Lucas. "Let's hope these assholes don't get slick and run a diagnostic check of the kid's body," Alexander stated.

Meanwhile, as Jeremiah turned on the flat screen TV, the entire Slade family glared at the news. The tragic scene of the horrific savagery at City Festival was being broadcasted.

"I would like to help," Nezera insisted. They all gazed at her standing in the middle of the living room.

"Don't you think you've done enough? This tragedy is a direct result of your actions. My secret was not yours to tell. You put Lucas in harm's way on purpose. Now, we must suffer the consequences. How am I supposed to ever trust you again?" Lori wept.

"I'm so sorry, Lo. I made a huge mistake out of anger. I know that now. I was only trying to protect you and this family," Nezera stressed.

"I don't need your protection. I am a big girl, capable of protecting myself. I don't know how many times I need to say it. Please stop trying to justify it. You might as well have hand-delivered Lucas to Ross. I am ashamed to call you my big sister!" Lori screamed, running out of the room.

With tears in her eyes, Nezera watched her sister leave the room. An unnatural silence came over them. "Come here, my girl. Just give her some time," Nora consoled, hugging Nezera.

"We have his signal!" Alexander shouted. They all flooded to the Research and Intel room. "The bio-beacon is weak, but we have the surrounding area. Interestingly enough, there's one industrial facility with underground access. Guess what...they own the property and we now have the address," Alexander explained.

"Alright, listen up people. The time for diplomacy is over. Grab every piece of tactical gear you have and load up. We need to grab these monsters before they move out with Lucas. Nez, Lucas loves Lori and he's now a part of this family. It's time to accept it and move on. We protect our family and those we love, but most importantly, we defend humanity against evil. So, we will stand together as a family, united as one coven…Silver-fangs," Joshua proclaimed. They stockpiled weapons and tactical gear, loaded their vehicles and headed out.

The Slades were hot on his trail when Lucas awakened to find himself strapped to a steel gurney. He could barely see, as bright lights beamed into his eyes.

"Welcome Mr. Shaw, to my home away from home. Feeling a little drowsy, are we?" Ross asked slyly.

"That's Captain Shaw, you asshole. How do you think I'm supposed to feel, you prick? The chloral hydrate was a nice touch though," Lucas taunted.

"Quick-witted with a slick tongue, huh boy? Just like your old man," Ross sneered.

"How dare you speak of my dad? You sadistic, inhuman, bloodsucking piece of scum. You slaughtered my mother and father!" Lucas shouted.

"Yes, I did and if I had to do it all over again, I would. You see, your father stole something very valuable from me. I financed his research and he betrayed me," Ross declared.

"No, you betrayed yourself and humanity. You're no pure-blood vampire, given the scar on your neck. My father created the cure to your nocturnal purgatory. He betrayed you because you wanted to bring about the end of the world. It seems the recurring goal for your sorry excuse of a species, is to walk in the daylight amongst the living. Look at you, you all are nothing but shades of your former selves," Lucas stated.

"You're brave, boy. You even managed to take out one of my best tonight," Ross admitted.

"Oh, I'm sorry. You mean ole' boy back at the store? If he was one of your best, that doesn't say a lot about your crew. You might be fast, strong and all that bullshit, but in the end, you're not invincible. I must say Dorian, I'm not impressed at all," Lucas admitted.

Grabbing Lucas by the throat, Ross stated, "I've had about all I can take of your big mouth, boy. Soon there will be no natural world and mankind will suffer the same fate as you, your parents, and those half-breeds you keep around as pets. Do you think they're so different from us? They are monsters pretending to be civil. The thirst affects them the same as us. How long will they ignore the hunger in their blood? I've slaughtered and fed on your kind, at will, for the last four hundred years. As unique as you may be, you are still inferior to me and my kind. Tonight, you were very lucky. But, I promise you, your luck has run its course," Ross threatened.

Lucas gazed at hi-tech canisters filled with blood...his blood.

"Yes, you see, we began extracting your blood and bone marrow while you were asleep. As you know, your blood cells are the key to our salvation. I assume the Sabers spoke of your purpose. See, you are nothing more than a failsafe your father bred, in order to safeguard the cure. His only success was buying mankind twenty-eight more years," Ross claimed.

"So, for your efforts, you will become the new Vampire High Guard Commander?" Lucas asked.

"Precisely, you understand the idea very well," Ross answered.

"Wow, you are truly a maniac. You're nothing more than a power-hungry, sadistic prick with fangs and a dumb ass, at that. I find it interesting, a pasty-face cracker is so gung-ho to be infused with nigga DNA. It might give you some brains, too," Lucas sneered.

Suddenly, the vampires became silent and gazed at their leader. Ross slowly turned around with a glare piercing from his cold, fierce blue eyes.

"You didn't even take the time to measure the correct dosage of chloral hydrate before loading it into the syringe. I can assure you, the amount you used was only enough to taint the blood you extracted from me. Good luck getting the chloral hydrate to run its course. You can keep that thousand-yard stare. You don't frighten me, nor do you impress me. I've fought and dealt with men like you before," Lucas declared.

"Lucas, what will silence you? You're captured, we now possess your body. Salvation is ours to claim. Your friends have failed at their pitiful attempts to protect you. Yet, you are still holding on to your hopes of a rescue. Now, I bet Joshua and his family would rather see you dead than try their attempt at another rescue. That would be a much easier win for them.

Personally, if I were in their shoes, I would simply put a bullet through the base of my skull and be done with it. You see, whether or not you choose to accept it, your days are numbered. Your life is forfeit. Like father like son," Ross taunted.

"Remember one thing, Ross. Whether or not you choose to accept it, in due time, I will run a blade through your throat and watch as you choke on the blood you have stolen from your victims," Lucas responded with a piercing glare of his own.

Ross laughed loudly as he turned to walk away.

As the sun lowered, the Slades continued to make their way toward Ross's location. With weapons armed and ready, Lori posed a relevant question to the family.

"How are we supposed to get within a mile of these bastards without them sniffing us out?" She asked.

"We will probably have to pull something out of our asses," Alexander said.

"We'll need a few fallback strategies. By now, they have Lucas's blood and bone marrow in vials ready for transport. Unknowingly, Lucas will temporarily lose his ability to regenerate and become more vulnerable than ever," Nora explained.

We'll have to destroy those vials and get Lucas out of there as best we can," Joshua explained.

"Do you think they've turned him?" Abigail asked.

"More than likely, no. They'll try and preserve every part of him as human. Ross won't risk tainting the cure. But, just in case, be prepared for anything and Lori, that goes double for you," Joshua stated.

"Give me ten minutes and I'll take the whole damn building down," Lori informed.

The facility where Lucas was being held, was connected to a small, abandoned airport. The vampires boarded the plane in preparation for a swift departure, as three guards stood on the lookout. With modified binoculars, Joshua, Nora, and Lori inspected the entire facility and surrounding area, while the others grabbed the weapons and gear from their vehicles.

"We need to take out their ride," Lori eagerly stated.

"How many are there?" Jeremiah asked.

"I have a headcount of fifteen men total. Three are standing guard by the plane and there's another twelve inside, including Ross," Lori replied. She was on point, not missing a single detail. Mentally, she was ready to walk through hell in order to rescue her man.

"Lo, take out the guards, secure the plane and wait for my instructions. Alex, you're our shooter, so locate higher ground and provide surveillance...watch our backs. Abby, feed us whatever Intel you can and monitor all frequencies. Nora, Jeremiah and I will move in on the warehouse. Nezera, secure this area and Abby," Joshua instructed.

Lori wasn't exactly pleased with Joshua's instructions. However, she understood the only way to succeed was to follow his orders and move as one unit. Joshua walked over to her and said, "I know you want to move in on the warehouse, but I need you focused. Root yourself in this very moment and in your faith. Nothing bad will become of Lucas. Secure the plane and wait for my signal. He placed a fatherly kiss to her forehead and proceeded. Nora put her arms around Lori attempting to ease her mind.

"Lo, we'll protect Lucas with every breath in our bodies. I promise you, everything will be just fine," Nora reassured.

As each of them moved into position, they began checking their ear communicators and securing the transponders.

Immediately, Lori moved in on Ross's men standing guard by the plane. She whipped the chain of her weapon and subdued her enemies, while slicing and cutting with the curved blade. She chopped up two guards within a matter of seconds, leaving a piles of fire and ash.

"Lori, what's your status?" Joshua inquired.

"Position one is secure," she responded.

"Damn, that girl is good," Jeremiah said.

"No, she's in love," Nora replied. The remaining henchmen were dispatched by Joshua, Nora and Jeremiah. They began deploying and utilizing a unique array of weaponry, turning each guard into ash. Alexander covered them from above with a high-powered rifle. Every bullet he fired was laced with silver nitrate.

"Lori, move into second position now," Joshua insisted.

She joined Joshua, Nora and Jeremiah. It seemed as if Ross and his henchmen were totally oblivious to what the Slades were doing on the outside. The storage facility was a very, large warehouse consisting of many access points. Ross felt the presence of intruders and radioed his guards to check in. However, the Slades were one step ahead. They had strategically rigged recording devices to the guard's transmission receivers, to appear as if each one was present and accounted for. Joshua, Nora and Jeremiah entered the warehouse from the ground. Joshua instructed Lori to enter the warehouse from above. Alexander instantly changed his position for a better vantage point on the warehouse.

"We have what we need. It's time to depart," Ross stated.

He instructed Drea to prepare the plane. Entering the warehouse, Joshua, Nora, and Jeremiah took up defensive positions and hid behind some old, storage equipment.

Joshua whispered into his communicator, "Alex, Drea is heading outside. The moment she's within range, take her out," Joshua ordered.

"Wait, I have my eyes on her. Let me have the pleasure," Lori pleaded.

"Okay Lo, but make it quick. After you take her out, we go live and you must return to your position overhead," Joshua explained.

Joshua, Nora and Jeremiah laced the warehouse with small detonators. These controlled explosives are designed to incinerate anyone within their proximity. As Drea set foot outside, she noticed small piles of fire and ash where each henchman once stood. Visibly disturbed by her surroundings, she angrily uttered through her fangs, "Those hybrid fucks." She drew her communicator to alert Ross, when suddenly, a steel chain rapped around her wrist, freeing her hand of the communicator. With light speed, an unforeseen adversary snatched Drea up and slammed her to the ground. Lori suddenly appeared overhead, as she retracted the steel chain.

"I've been waiting for this, you hybrid bitch. Came to rescue your mortal lover, huh? How romantic," Drea uttered sarcastically.

"Yes, and to kill you," Lori replied, before unleashing her weapon as an extension of her rage.

Maintaining the upper hand, Lori moved swifter and more efficient than ever. While a violent rage of love and passion coursed through her veins, she quickly outpaced Drea, dispatching her in a matter of minutes. Lori whirled the chain around her neck, choking her as the curved dagger slit her throat. Drea's head suddenly detached from her body and blood gushed from the base of her neck. Her body combusted into ashes and flames, reducing her to nothing. Lori's predatory eyes blazed with fury, as her fangs elongated.

"Lo, you are one bad bitch, my sister," Alexander stated gazing into his sniper scope.

"Damn right," she replied.

"Lori, are you back in position?" Joshua asked.

"I am in position, copy," she answered.

Ross sensed something was off. His protection detail wasn't answering, when all of a sudden, he caught the scent of the hybrids.

"They're here! Lock and load!" He yelled.

His men began grabbing ammunition and automatic rifles, preparing a shootout with the Slades.

"Secure the boy. The rest of you, follow me," Ross ordered. They quickly left the subterranean level and confronted the Slades.

"Have you and your family come to die, Joshua?" Ross sneered.

"We've come for the boy. Give us Lucas and we walk away. I strongly believe you should consider my offer," Joshua stated.

They continued to trade words during the stand-off. "Consider this, you hybrid misfits!" Ross shouted, while he and his men blasted endless rounds of fire.

"Prepare to go live on my mark…5-4-3-2-1," Joshua ordered, while pushing the remote detonator on his watch. Each magnetic, explosive device contained eight ounces of garlic and metallic silver, combined with C4 explosives. After the detonation, every vampire in the vicinity collapsed, while silver and garlic filled the atmosphere. Their skin began to burn, as the silver and garlic infected their immune systems. The Slades brutally returned fire on every vampire. The device that exploded closest to Ross, grazed the left side of his face. It took him down long enough for Lori to maneuver to the subterranean level.

"Abby, have you accessed their system?" Lori asked on the communicator.

"Your timing is impeccable, sis. I just did. There are five more men on the subterranean," Abigail stated.

"Ok, work on finding me an alternate exit. I doubt we'll make it back to the surface," Lori said.

As Lori hurried underground, she unleashed her deadly fury. Maneuvering and killing every one of Ross's guards and henchmen with her automatic pistol and chained weapon.

11

The Captain's Final Solution

Struggling to free himself, Lucas remained strapped to the metal gurney. After killing the last guard at the door, Lori rushed in and found her beloved. Sudden relief fell over him. His eyes watered at the sight of his beautiful savior.

"Oh, thank God. I was beginning to think you'd forgotten me," Lucas said.

"I would never, ever do that, my love," Lori answered.

She quickly ripped off the restraints and hugged him tightly. She looked deep into his eyes, as they proceeded to kiss passionately.

"That's one hell of a welcome, Ms. Slade," Lucas said.

Lori handed him the assault rifle and insisted, "We must leave now."

"I have the package...I repeat, I have the package. We're moving to a secondary extraction point. Abby, I need to know where the tunnel leads us to. We must find an exit," Lori insisted. As they fled the room, Lori tossed a grenade...completely destroying the entire area.

Containing the situation above, Joshua and the rest of the family concluded the mop up. Unfortunately, Dorian Ross was nowhere to be found. Meanwhile, Lori and Lucas continued into the darkness, while combing through the maze of tunnels.

"Lo, the tunnel will continue for two miles before you reach a manhole. Soon, we'll lose radio contact. You need to make it to that manhole as soon as possible. I'll be waiting there. Also, the family is unable to locate Ross. He must have slipped away during the battle. I would get a move on, if I were you," Abigail urged.

"Stay very close to me, Lucas. I'll lead us out of here," Lori stated. They continued to make their way through the dark tunnels. While in search of the backup extraction point, Lori sensed the presence of vampires.

"Wait here," she whispered to Lucas.

He immediately knew what she was implying. More vampires lurked in the darkness. Lori disappeared as Lucas stood pointing his rifle, realizing he was the bait.

Suddenly, a vampire lashed out causing Lucas to flinch. Lori instantly intercepted as she immerged from the darkness. Using her Kyoketsu Shoge weapon, she stabbed, slashed and sliced the vampire. He was pinned against the wall, bleeding profusely, then turned to ashes. While catching her breath, she uttered, "We need to keep moving." Eventually, they approached an abandoned sub-terrain facility. Lori reached out and grabbed Lucas.

"What is it?" He whispered.

"The extraction point is a half-mile above us. Abigail and Nezera will be waiting for you. Use the stairs, then the manhole to get out," Lori instructed.

"Hell no! I'm not leaving you down here to fight these bastards," Lucas shouted.

"Look, there's no time. Please go, Lucas," she said, turning her attention to the dreadful hissing sounds surrounding them.

Lucas leaned and kissed her briefly. "Listen, just keep moving and we'll find you, no matter where you are," he declared. He followed her instructions and made his way up the stairs to the manhole. Lori stood her ground, taking up a defensive posture as she jerked the chain her Kyoketsu Shoge. As more growling and hissing came from the darkness, multiple vicious figures were crawling on the walls and creeping from behind the structures. Suddenly, Lori recognized a distinct voice. "Little Siren, how sweet," Ross sneered. Half of his face scorched from exposure to the silver and garlic blasts. Wielding her weapon, Lori began killing most of the vampires, as Ross trailed close behind her. She managed to escape. Meanwhile, Lucas found Abigail and Nezera.

"Do you have Lori on GPS?" He asked.

"Yes. She's above ground and moving very quickly," Abigail explained.

"Where is she now, Lucas? Why did you leave her?" Nezera yelled.

"Listen, we don't have time for your shit, Nez. I pleaded with her to let me stay, but she gave me no choice. She insisted I leave," Lucas said angrily.

Lori was battered and bleeding, yet she still managed to fend off the vampires chasing her. As she battled Ross, a car crashed into them. Unharmed, Ross towered over Lori. He kicked her in the stomach, as she laid helpless on the pavement. Ross was about to eliminate Lori, when Nezera hit him with the van, tossing him a great distance. Lucas leaped out the van and pulled Lori inside. Nezera quickly pulled off, as Lucas began to assess Lori's cuts and lacerations. Her face was covered in blood. Lori sustained a deep laceration to her abdomen and was bleeding out. Lucas attempted to cut his wrist and feed her some blood, when Lori grabbed his arm.

"No," she murmured.

"Lori please, you're bleeding out…you're bleeding to death," Lucas begged.

"I don't care. I won't let you," she insisted and passed out.

"Lucas, there are blood packs in the freezer case," Abigail stated.

Lucas frantically opened the case and tore open a pack. He fed Lori the blood, while Abigail applied bandages and dressings to her wounds. He held Lori in his arms, as she consumed a few packs within a matter of seconds. Meanwhile, they gazed deeply into each other's eyes. It was apparent, their love knew no bounds.

"How's she doing?" Nezera asked.

"She has fallen asleep and her wounds are healing nicely. Tough, brave, beautiful and loyal...what more can one man ask for?" He smiled and placed a gentle kiss on Lori's forehead. Finally, they arrived home. Joshua, Nora, and the others joined them shortly thereafter. Lucas took Lori in his arms and carried her to her room, gently placing her on the bed.

"How much blood has she lost?" Nora asked.

"A lot. She downed five or six blood packs before she fell asleep," Lucas answered.

While nursing Lori's wounds, Nora noticed she began healing instantly.

"Give her a few hours. She'll be fine and her wounds are healing very quickly. Lo just needs to rest for now," Nora proclaimed.

"If you don't mind, I'd like to stay with her," Lucas expressed.

As the rest of the family left the room, Nora remained behind observing the look of sadness on Lucas's face.

"She risked her life for me and yet, I feel so powerless," Lucas expressed.

"At times, Lori can be tough as nails, but she's very vulnerable when it comes to you. I've never seen her like this. You both need each other's love and protection," Nora explained.

She endearingly touched Lucas on his shoulder before leaving. He gently planted a kiss on Lori's lips and for a brief moment, her eyes opened as Lucas wiped the blood from her face. Kneeling beside her, he expressed his undying love. He also vowed to always protect and honor her.

"I can't even begin to explain the events I have experienced in the last few weeks. Vampires, Day-walkers, Reoccurrences, and Super-soldiers all existed in tales of fantasy, so I thought. My feelings for you and the connection we share are unexplainable. What I know is, you're the most precious thing to me. You have opened my heart to a level I never thought was attainable. My dark flashbacks and nightmares don't seem so bad, as long as you're in my life. I need you

to understand what I have to do, babe." Lucas professed. He gently kissed Lori and left the room.

He stepped onto the patio and pondered his next steps. Directly confronting Ross would be the only way to trap him long enough for the Slades to obliterate him and his crew. Lucas hurried quietly to the garage and gathered two battle rifles, a few silver stakes, and a machete. His phone rang in the process and the number on the caller ID was unknown. He slowly placed the phone to his ear. The voice on the other end was familiar, yet ghastly, "Captain Shaw."

"I'm not going to ask how you got my number," Lucas said angrily.

"Are you still hiding behind your little bitch and her family of hybrid misfits, Lucas? We have pressing business to handle. I don't care how long it takes, even if I have to burn this entire city to the fucking ground. You will give me what I want," Ross declared.

"You know something, Dorian? You don't have to worry much longer because I'm coming for you. I'll promise you two things…one, you will never get what you want unless you kill me first and two, nothing or no one will stop me from ripping your fucking nuts off," Lucas promised.

"You are very presumptuous for a mortal. Good…not too smart, but good. Your father was the exact same. Until he was begging for your beautiful mother's life, while me and my crew took turns raping her. I tore his head from his body. What makes you think you're equipped to fight me on your own?" Ross asked.

"As you already know, I'm no ordinary mortal and I'm no stranger to killing. Most importantly, I'm not my father," Lucas declared.

"No, you're not, but you can still die the same horrific death. I might even make you watch as we slaughter your little girlfriend and her family," Ross assured.

"We shall see, Dorian. I know you must be running out of minions by now," Lucas taunted.

"Not a problem, Mr. Shaw. I have more than enough men to finish my mission. Let's quit stalling, Captain. I presume you already know my location," Ross stated.

"Yeah, I got it asshole," Lucas answered.

"Will your friends be joining us, or will you die alone like the weak, pathetic mortal you are?" Ross asked.

"Being mortal doesn't make me weak. I'll see you real soon, you fake-ass, Deacon Frost wannabe!" Lucas shouted and hung up. Just as he ended the call, Joshua walked in looking very perplexed. Lucas proceeded to explain, "I already know what you're going to say, but I have to end this now. I almost lost her tonight, Josh. I've never felt more helpless in my entire life. Ross will not stop until he gets what he wants."

"She has been waiting for you for a very, very long time, Luc. The moment she saw you, her heart nearly stopped. Are you sure you want to do this?" Joshua asked.

"I'm damn sure. Besides, you all have me on GPS. I'll kill as many of them as I can, while buying you some time. Do you have any detonators? I can rig the place to blow and that can be your signal," Lucas explained.

"You want to use yourself as bait? Lori won't like this one bit," Joshua pleaded.

"Yeah I know, but this has to be done. We can't keep battling Ross throughout this city putting more innocent lives at risk, including your family," Lucas explained.

"Lucas, we are who we are. This is not the first time we've dealt with a psychopathic immortal. I see more of your father in you every day," Joshua said.

Lucas acknowledged Joshua's kind words and continued out the door. "Hey kid, take the G-Wagon and remember to park it out of sight. We still have payments to make on that ride," Joshua chuckled.

He was very impressed by Lucas's initiative and courage to change up the game. "At last, our family is complete and the last piece of the puzzle has been found. A man well-worth the gift of immortality," Joshua whispered proudly.

12

Killcount Arises

Ross secured another warehouse facility that was off the beaten path. Now, armed with only a dozen men, he had expected a trap. Knowing Lori was asleep and recovering, Lucas realized he needed to do this for her. The images of Ross violently stomping Lori on the ground, as she lay beaten and hurt, continued to plague Lucas's mind. Not to mention, he was still rehashing the violent memories of his parents' death.

"No way will you live after tonight, no way motherfucker," Lucas said angrily, as he drove away.

Knowing the vampires could sniff him out within a mile radius, Lucas had to move quickly. Lacing the warehouse with booby traps and death devices was not easy. However, given the vastness of the warehouse, he would have a twenty-minute window before Ross and his men would close in. Lucas heavily relied on his abilities learned in the Military such as, stealth and guerilla warfare tactics. In addition to, planting tripwires, directional land mines and improvised explosive devices (IED). This would buy him some time, as he awaited the Slades' arrival.

Back at residence, Lori awakened just in time to join the rest of the family, as they prepared for their final assault. The fierce creature within had exposed itself, as her gashes and cuts healed instantly.

"Where is he?" She said angrily, revealing her predatory features.

"Lucas left. He wanted to buy us time, as you regained your strength. We have a plan in place, but we must go now," Joshua explained.

"Foolish boy," Lori huffed, as her fangs elongated.

The entire Slade coven left in route to the warehouse. Lori and Nezera sat in the back seat.

"I am happy for you, little sister. I was afraid you would let down your guard and risk your life. For as long as I can remember, I've always taken care of you. I can't help but feel responsible. I now see, you have a man who worships, adores and protects you by any means. I can see it in his eyes. Please forgive me for my weakness," Nezera begged.

"I love you too, sis," Lori said softly.

Meanwhile, Lucas positioned himself in the proper vicinity allowing his scent to linger. Like lambs to the slaughter, Ross and his henchmen moved toward the death traps. As the tripwires and explosives detonated, the silver engulfed the atmosphere. It began to scorch, kill and maim the vampires. Using his rifles and firearms, Lucas proceeded to blast every vampire within his path. He burned them by using ultraviolet ammunition, turning them into piles of ash. The other devices impaled the vampires with silver and wooden stakes. In the midst of the firefight, Joshua contacted Lucas. The Slades had arrived.

"Lucas, Lucas are you there?" Joshua beckoned.

"Yep, I'm alive for the moment," Lucas replied, breathing heavily.

"We are in position. Can you come to the west side of the warehouse?" Joshua asked.

"Yes, but I have one more trick to perform. How's Lori?" Lucas asked.

"She's a tad bit ticked off," Joshua stated.

"Luc, the moment we get out of here, I plan to kick your ass. I still love you, though. Now, get your ass over here," Lori demanded.

"The two of you sound like an old, married couple," Alexander joked.

Low on ammo, Lucas plays his last trick. He sets off a large UV blast, incinerating every single bloodsucker. To avoid the blast, Ross and his lieutenants dove for cover. Cycling his rifle, Lucas was down to one last magazine. It's only a matter of time before he gets up-close and personal, drawing his machete. Without breaking stride, Lucas hauled ass towards the Slades' location using the UV blast as cover. Lori and the rest of the family intercepted Lucas. Ross continued to pursue his prize, with hopes of obliterating the Slade Clan.

"Shaw, you lucky son of a bitch!" Ross yelled, realizing he'd been outwitted.

He continued taunting Lucas about the death of his parents, hoping for a one-on-one confrontation.

"You best end me tonight or I will track down and slaughter everyone you care about. I will bathe in and drink the blood of those you love…starting with your little Siren girlfriend," Ross threatened.

Lori grabbed Lucas before he could retaliate.

"Luc, you can't. You are no match for him. Don't you even think about it," she pleaded.

"Well, I'm definitely not letting you go. For too long, this maniac has haunted my dreams and lived without consequence for my parents' death. This ends right here and right now!" Lucas shouted.

"Well, I'm coming with you," Lori demanded.

Alexander offers Lucas his rifle, allowing him to blast his way to Ross. The rest of the family began fighting their way through the warehouse. Each Hunter utilized their own signature weaponry and fighting skills, while detonating explosives and destroying the warehouse. Meanwhile, Lucas and Lori tag teamed and commenced to dispatch the majority of vampires in the process. While fighting, they became separated and Lucas continued to pursue Ross.

They meet again. Without delay, Lucas began hacking, swinging and delivering numerous melee attacks. He realized he was in for the fight of his life. Ross was a far more superior opponent and fighter with enhanced strength, agility and reflexes. Even his momentum was augmented, allowing him to propel Lucas at a lengthy distance. Ross maintained the upper hand in their duel. However, Lucas continued to show courage and resilience, struggling to hold his own. Lucas had grown stronger and more enhanced while combating Ross. He displayed heightened endurance, reflexes and pain suppression. This allowed him to take extreme punishment from Ross. Even the most grievous of wounds and injuries did not impair Lucas. Eventually, his efforts overwhelmed Ross, sending him flying several feet away with brute force of a single kick.

"You're a lot tougher than I thought, boy. Much tougher than your ole man," Ross provoked.

Continuing to duel, Ross was able to counter Lucas's abilities. He tossed him into a pile of old warehouse materials and debris. Before Ross could deliver another attack, Lori grabbed his wrist using her signature weapon. She launched Ross away from Lucas. Surprised and off balance, Ross couldn't outmaneuver her blade and chain weapon. She wielded it with amazing precision and accuracy, using the weapon as an extension of her body. Lori steadily maintained her momentum. She quickly struck his hand and severed his fingers. She then struck his other hand and penetrated the blade through the middle...leaving him completely helpless. She suddenly tied him up, bound his hands, and forced Ross onto the blade. As Lucas regained his strength, he noticed Lori struggling to attempt her final *coup de gras*. Rising to his feet, Lucas grabbed his machete. He made an incredible leap, bounced off a cylinder pillar, and violently pierced the blade into Ross's neck. At last, Ross met his defeat. His death was just as brutal and gruesome as his many victims. His body instantly disintegrated into fiery ashes, leaving nothing but a mound of bones and debris.

Lucas and Lori had finally rid themselves of the monster who plagued they're lives. They devotedly looked at each other in a state of relief.

"Are you okay?" Lucas asked.

Before Lori could respond, Lucas's knees buckled, and he collapsed to the ground. Lori quickly rushed to his aid, supporting his head and neck. His body wasn't recovering instantaneously, due to the extraction of bone marrow. His other para-enhanced abilities functioned normally, but his healing factor was stunted for the time being. Given the severity of his wounds, the damage could kill him. The rest of the family finally caught up after dispatching Ross's minions. Nora rushed to Lucas's side with a syringe and a miniature vile of medication.

"I was afraid this was going to happen. Lo, we have to keep him awake long enough for the medication to work. Luc, I'm injecting you with an enzyme boost. It will jumpstart the healing process. Your blood will clot, but you have to stay awake for us, okay?" Nora explained.

"Sounds fantastic," Lucas replied softly.

"You've been brave enough for one day, my love. Just listen to my voice and keep your eyes open," Lori pleaded.

Lucas was beginning to drift in and out of consciousness, while the medication ran its course. Lori lightly smacked his face, attempting to keep him awake.

"This can't be goodbye. Just hold on, baby…please," she cried.

13

A Strange New World

In the aftermath of the destruction, bright lights emerged from the sky. The noise of a military helicopter and other aerial vehicles descended upon the warehouse that was ablaze from the fire fight. The Colonel emerged from the chopper. His private militia arrived soon thereafter, taking possession of his grandson. A medic and a transport was onsite, ready for immediate evacuation. Lucas's blood began to clot, although his wounds took a while to fully heal. Nora requested the Colonel transport Lucas to the N.I.G.H.T.F.A.L.L. substation, where their state-of-the-art, medical facility was located. The Colonel agreed, wanting his grandson to receive the best care available. Interestingly, he seemed very familiar with the N.I.G.H.T.F.A.L.L. operations. Lori refused to leave Lucas's side and on the way to the substation, she professed her eternal love. She explained she'd waited nearly three hundred years for his return. She caressed his hand in the helicopter, while sitting next to the Colonel and Nora. The Colonel became sympathetic to the bond they shared. Lucas gazed at Lorelei's beautiful face, before falling into a deep and much-needed sleep. He rested peacefully, knowing he had honored his parents by destroying his archenemy.

In his dream, Lucas awakened face down in a field of grass, as the sun blared. He could hear the sound of her voice calling out to him.

"Lucas, Lucas, it's alright. I'm here...I'm right here with you," Lori assured. She took his hand, as he rose to his feet. Her face was as lovely as ever and Lucas was totally captivated by the very sight of her.

"Where are we? Am I dead?" He asked.

"No, babe. You are very much alive and resting comfortably," Lori explained.

"Lo, is this a dream? How did you appear?" Lucas asked bewildered.

"Remember the first night we met? I asked if you believed in the supernatural," Lori recalled.

"Yes, I remember," Lucas answered.

"Babe, we share a connection even I can't explain. I have no idea how this is possible, but I'm loving every minute of it," Lori expressed gleefully.

"Yes...I feel it, too. Lo, no matter where I am, as long as I'm with you, I couldn't care less," Lucas professed and they kissed passionately.

Somehow, the strength of their connection allowed them to enter each other's minds...a dream-sharing experience. They continued walking and the field suddenly transformed into a plantation. It was the exact place they'd met centuries ago. Lori was eager to reveal everything to Lucas just as she'd promised.

Lucas abruptly awakened several hours later with an IV in his arm. He lifted his shirt and noticed all of his wounds had vanished. Afterwards, the Colonel and Nora entered the room. She had treated Lucas, along with the medical staff. Due to her endless efforts, his accelerated healing abilities were completely restored.

"How are you feeling, kid?" The Colonel asked.

"I feel great, considering the circumstances," Lucas replied in jest.

The Colonel embraced Lucas and said, "I thought I'd lost you, my boy. Job well done, son…job well done."

"How long was I out?" Lucas asked.

"Luc, you were on bedrest for two days. It's great to have you back," Nora smiled.

I certainly appreciate everything you've done, Doc. I can't thank you enough," Lucas expressed.

"You're most certainly welcome, Captain. You're a remarkable man and Lo has chosen a fine companion," Nora beamed.

Before she could complete her sentence, the rest of the Slade clan burst through the door, ecstatic to see Lucas. Even Nezera exhibited newfound concern and feelings for him.

"Luc, I need to apologize for my vindictiveness and ill-will. I was concerned for my sister and didn't want to see her hurt again. Because of you, I'm reminded of who my sister truly is…a beautiful sunflower who loves you unconditionally, come hell or high-water," Nezera acclaimed.

"Brother, you must have some serious steel running through your veins. You not only took out a vampire, but a powerful Blood-Lord. That requires some really big balls to accomplish," Jeremiah commended.

Abigail rushed to Lucas, gave him a big, sisterly hug and said, "Luc, it's great to see you've recovered."

"Well damn, babe. How can you tell? You got him all hemmed up and shit," Alexander joked.

"We're all grateful you pulled through, man. I knew you'd take care of business with that rifle I gave you," Alexander said.

Everyone was there to celebrate Lucas, except Lori. Joshua shook Lucas's hand and welcomed him as a new addition to his family.

"You've done the impossible and no one could have done it better, Lucas," Joshua stated.

"Well, I had a good teacher," Lucas responded.

The colossal-sized man who stood next to Joshua began to speak. "The word is quickly spreading and you definitely set the tone, kid. I can only imagine what you could accomplish, if you were one of us," he stated.

"Lucas, I would like to introduce you to Kaleb Sloan, the Chief Operations Officer and Director of *N.I.G.H.T.F.A.L.L.* He's also the patriarch and leader of the Midwest Coven," Joshua explained.

"It's an honor to meet you, Mr. Sloan. You're one of the Saber Lords, along with Joshua…Iron-Fang Sloan," Lucas stated. Everyone in the room was shocked by his familiarity with Kaleb.

"I see someone has been reading the ancient text," Kaleb said.

By this time, the Colonel had long left the room. Lucas became very interested in the location of the facility and the many references to *N.I.G.H.T.F.A.L.L.*

"Josh, do you mind if I borrow your young prodigy? He needs to be brought up to speed. That is, if you think he's ready to receive the trade secrets," Kaleb inquired.

"This brother is thorough…a great listener and very attentive. Furthermore, he's no stranger to handling government secrets," Joshua stated. Lucas gladly left the room with Kaleb, elated about his exposure to a whole new era...where legend, myth, and nightmares exist.

"I heard references to *N.I.G.H.T.F.A.L.L.* a few years ago when I was in the military. What sort of operation is this?" Lucas asked.

"Well, as you may know, we're not your typical, run-of-the-mill intelligence agency. During WWII, a paranormal event occurred that could have obliterated the very texture of reality and no one was the wiser. The catastrophic event was averted, evidence sealed, and those baring witness to it, were sworn to secrecy. In the wake of that event, the government, along with extraordinary factions, formed an experimental subsidiary program known as *Nocturnal Operations* or *Noc-Ops*," Kaleb explained.

"The program enlisted the assistance of various para-human individuals who stood for equality and justice. Utilizing their incredible capabilities, they sought to bridge the gap between worlds. In 2021, multiple governments passed a bill to enact the *Paranormal Defense Initiative*. They required the para-cursed, the augmented, and the strange to be monitored. I say, fuck that. We'll only monitor those who pose a threat to national and international security.

We would work with the Armed Forces and receive funding from those governments but remain a private organization with no political ties or motivations. Our primary concern is to keep a close reign on those who threaten the sanctity of the natural world. The moment those persons, entities or factions step out of line, we intervene. Our cause is pure and to hell with politics and all that other bullshit. We need men like yourself, Captain. We need heroes," Kaleb stated.

As a Hybrid-Lord, Kaleb has lived for centuries. His personality was very large and serious, which paired very well with his muscular stature. He also exhibited great character. Although Kaleb was uncompromising, direct and lethal...he was also kind, trustworthy and extremely courageous. As well as, a wonderful sense of humor.

"Welcome to the N.I.G.H.T.F.A.L.L. regime, Captain," Kaleb announced. The headquarters was massive, unlike any other intelligence network Lucas had encountered. The facility was located in Houston, Texas, with substations in Atlanta, Maryland (Andrews Air Force Base) and Los Angeles. In addition, N.I.G.H.T.F.A.L.L. has multiple bases in England, Canada, Dubai, Malaysia and Japan. The regime possessed advanced, cutting-edge technology. Their intel and communications equipment was second-to-none. Holographic displays filled the briefing rooms with visual analyst, projections of digital mapping and facial reconstructs. The weapons and tactical gear were highly enhanced. Each level contained its very own Quarter Master, who trained operatives and personnel on weaponry and tactical equipment utilization. The facility concealed approximately ten stories below ground. The top-level contained offices and memorials of fallen operatives. The ground base opened at surface level to allow hovercrafts and planes to depart safely, while transporting operatives to their designated locations.

Kaleb informed Lucas of his family's huge stake in the N.I.G.H.T.F.A.L.L. regime. Surprisingly, Lucas's parents were primary benefactors of the agency and his father held a position on the Board of Trustees during its founding days. The Colonel, Lucas's grandfather, served as a military liaison between N.I.G.H.T.F.A.L.L. and the Armed Forces. Instantly, the pieces began to fall into place, as Lucas realized the close connection between the Slades and his parents.

"After your parents died, the agency felt a grave loss, Lucas. We all mourned for days on end," Kaleb explained. As they came upon a training hall, Lucas noticed Lori instructing a class of recruits. She was teaching extremely difficult lessons in armed and unarmed combat. After Kaleb concluded his introduction to N.I.G.H.T.F.A.L.L., he politely excused himself. Suddenly, a mysterious, older woman appeared by Lucas's side.

"Magnificent, isn't she?" The woman said.

"She's extraordinary," Lucas replied.

"Yes, she is. She's waited many, many lifetimes to reunite with you. The bond you share will ultimately define your lives. Together, you will possess the strength and ability to accomplish anything…to defeat all enemies," the woman proclaimed.

"And how do you know this?" He asked with skepticism.

"Lucas, you might say I'm a seer…a prophet of sorts," she stated. He was totally stunned when she addressed him by name.

"Tumbling down the rabbit hole, I see," she said sarcastically.

"Ma'am, you have no idea. I actually thought I knew the shadows and dark places of this world. I now realize everything and everyone are just smoke and mirrors," Lucas said.

"Not everyone, Lucas. When gazing into her eyes, do you see shades of darkness or a fulfilling, bright future together?" The woman inquired.

"Lori entered into my dreams as I slept," Lucas disclosed.

"You have the ability to do the same, if you so desire. The love that binds you two is very powerful and it extends beyond time or reason," the woman professed.

"What is she...who is she?" Lucas asked.

"She is your soul's counterpart desperately seeking to become whole. You know what I speak of. You can feel it. The irresistible, uncontrollable attraction you can't explain. The pounding of your heart when she enters the room...the tingle up your spine when she touches you," she described. The wise woman urged Lucas to claim his everlasting love for Lori and to never look back. But before Lucas could respond, she had vanished.

After Lori's training class, she approached Lucas and began flirting heavily. She tugged on his belt, closing the distance between them and kissed his lips.

"Wanna go a few rounds?" She teased. Lucas laughed and said, "Honey, you have no idea."

"Oh yeah...what exactly did you have in mind, Captain?" Lori asked seductively.

Without hesitation, Lucas led Lori into a vacant auxiliary room. He positioned her on a countertop and placed his head between her legs. Sliding her panties to the side, he slowly ran his tongue across Lori's pearl.

"Fuck...oh fuck. I see you want to tame me, Captain," she moaned, biting her bottom lip. Lori held his head in place, as her juices flowed down his chin. With each stroke of Lucas's tongue, Lori sermonized in multiple languages. As her Siren-like features manifested, she held his face close. Using her long, forked tongue, she licked her sweet nectar from his lips. In a state of intense passion, she stripped Lucas's pants down to his ankles. Taking his shaft in her hand, she ran her tongue across the tip and took him deep into her mouth. She loved giving, as well as receiving.

Lucas quickly positioned Lori against the wall. He began thrusting his shaft into her wetness, as she locked her legs tightly around his waist. The pleasure they shared knew no bounds. Lori turned around so Lucas could enter her from the back. She was falling deeper and deeper in love with every stroke. They could no longer control themselves, as they began to climax. It was as if the world had stopped on its axis. Lucas and Lori held each other closely, kissing deeply.

"Are you trying to break me down, Captain? Damn, that was amazing," Lori expressed.

"My desire is to enjoy every part of you, Ms. Slade. I'm falling so hard for you and I've never felt this way before," Lucas explained.

"Shhhh...don't say another word, my love. I can see it in your eyes and the eyes don't lie. I love you, too," Lori professed. They could hardly contain the joy they felt, as they were getting dressed. Shortly thereafter, they explored the halls of the facility. Lori turned to look at Lucas and said, "I'm considering resigning as an operative. This has been my life for over two hundred years. Living in the shadows...hunting, killing and always feeling alone. I'm very good at it. Hell, I'm the best at it. But, I'm still half-human. I want to turn off the beast and experience something more, if only for a little while. Besides, who's going to watch your ass, if I am constantly answering calls to save the world?"

"Well, I must say, you do an excellent job of watching my ass, but are you sure this is what you want? I know how hard it is to lay down the sword after clutching it for so long. Eventually, it calls out to you...it never forgets your name," Lucas stated.

"I didn't get into this life to save the world, Lucas. I did it to disguise my inner feelings. I didn't want to hurt people, but the angry beast inside was hungry. I thought feeding it would lessen the pain of being human. Babe, I'm so ready to leave that life behind me. It's a new dawn, it's a new day. It's a new life for me and I'm feeling good," Lori said joyfully.

"Nina Simone, right?" Lucas replied.

"That's right...I absolutely love her music," Lori admitted and while holding hands, they walked out of the front door and into the night. Over the next few months, Lucas completed college and earned his degree. He and Lori moved in together and were forever inseparable.

Eventually, the Slades relocated to their home in Atlanta, Georgia and the timing couldn't have been more perfect. Lucas was accepted into Morehouse College to pursue his Master's degree. Nora continued mentoring Lucas, helping him to excel beyond his expectations. Meanwhile, Lori submitted her resignation as a N.I.G.H.T.F.A.L.L. operative, but continued serving the initiative as a per diem instructor. She also accepted a Librarian position at Spellman College, so she could remain close to her man. Before the fall semester began, Lucas and Lori spent the entire summer traveling. They visited New York, L.A., Las Vegas, Miami and London. As well as, the Eastern Covens of Dubai and Kuala Lumpur, Malaysia. The Slades owned multiple properties throughout the world, so the possibilities were endless. For centuries, they had accumulated a vast fortune and unlimited resources. The Slades always took very good care of their own.

Lucas and Lorelei were the happiest they'd ever been. For the first time in their lives, they could finally experience the sweet taste of freedom, that which a past of violence had denied for centuries. All of their accounts were balanced, and their pasts forgiven.

At least, so they thought.

About the Author

Quentin T. Barrett is an aspiring new author who

is motivated to tell his narratives in the genre of

Sci-fi/Fantasy Urban Thrillers. He is an experienced

Martial Artist and a member of the International

Shuri-Te Yudansha-Kai. Quentin earned his

Bachelor of Science degree in Graphic
Communications

from North Carolina A&T State University. He is also

an action film and comic book enthusiast.